Praise for *Too Glorious to Even Long for on Certain Days*

"In his beautifully written novella, *Too Glorious to Even Long for on Certain Days*, Joseph Bathanti delivers a moving meditation on memory and the truth an individual finds in life. With Camus looming large in the young narrator, Fritz's mind, we see parallels to *The Stranger* as well as 'The Myth of Sisyphus' as we are introduced to the various characters and situations of his life. While working in a toy warehouse, he tells us he spends his time 'reassembling tiny broken worlds,' and later suggests that 'memory is the rock we bully up the hill.' There are lines and descriptions to savor on every page and the whole of this stellar work will leave the reader immensely satisfied and also thinking of their own truths and the broken worlds they have witnessed along the way."

—Jill McCorkle, author of *Life After Life*

"It is a rare and special artist who compels readers to yearn for the well-being of their characters as deeply and as tenderly as Joseph Bathanti makes us yearn for his. These familiar friends and relatives and lovers—

burdened with desire heavier than the boulder that owns Sisyphus—possess a spiritual stamina that is their blessing and their curse. They earn our empathy while they push against dead-end jobs, the weight of family, and otherworldly spells of love. Life-changing questions illuminate the periphery of every nuanced scene. The sublime inhabits these pages too, a wide-eyed wonder at the danger our protagonist insists on moving toward. Bathanti's craftsmanship is a work of magic that leaves us embracing the mystery of how such flawed and complicated humans can make us feel more forgiving, more merciful, more alive. *Too Glorious to Even Long for on Certain Days* is a powerful work of art that forces us to slow down, to hold close every loved one who will, too soon, disappear."

—Matt Cashion, author of *Last Words of the Holy Ghost*

"*Too Glorious to Even Long For on Certain Days* captures nineteen-year-old Fritz Sweeney on the cusp of adulthood, a time when one decision can chart a life's course. In this vivid and absorbing novella, Joseph Bathanti grapples with big questions about work, love, family, faith, forgiveness, belonging, and how much we can hope for from life. This is a book about possibilities, what worlds to enter, what paths to go down, and what doors to shut. I loved spending time with Fritz during the summer of 1973 in Pittsburgh, a city that bursts alive through the beauty and specificity of Bathanti's prose. Bathanti portrays complex and real characters in a full and pulsing world in this novella; *Too Glorious to Even Long for on Certain Days* is a feat of compression and a masterclass in characterization."

—Karin Lin-Greenberg, author of *You Are Here*

the summer of 1973 in Pittsburgh, a city that bursts alive through the beauty and specificity of Bathanti's prose. Bathanti portrays complex and real characters in a full and pulsing world in this novella; *Too Glorious to Even Long for on Certain Days* is a feat of compression and a masterclass in characterization."

—Karin Lin-Greenberg, author of *You Are Here*

Too Glorious to Even Long for on Certain Days

Joseph Bathanti

Regal House Publishing

Copyright © 2025 Joseph Bathanti. All rights reserved.

Published by
Regal House Publishing, LLC
Raleigh, NC 27605
All rights reserved

ISBN -13 (paperback): 9781646036158
ISBN -13 (epub): 9781646036165

Cover images and design by © studiochi.art

The author and Regal House Publishing extend gratitude to Penguin Random House for the permission to quote from the following texts: *The Stranger*, by Albert Camus, published by Vintage Book, 1942, translated by Stuart Gilbert, cover illustration by Leo Lionni; and "The Myth of Sisyphus," by Albert Camus, translated by Justin O'Brien, from *Existentialism from Dostoevsky to Sartre*, edited by Walter Kaufmann, published by Meridian Books, 1956.

The following is a work of fiction created by the author. All names, individuals, characters, places, items, brands, events, etc. are either the product of the author's imagination or are used fictitiously. Any resemblance to actual events, places, institutions, persons, current or past, is entirely coincidental.

All rights reserved. No part of this publication may be reproduced, stored in a retrieval system, or transmitted, in any form or by any means, electronic, mechanical, photocopying, recording, or otherwise, without the prior permission of Regal House Publishing.

Regal House Publishing supports rights of free expression and the value of copyright. The purpose of copyright is to encourage the creation of artistic works that enrich and define culture.

Printed in the United States of America

Regal House Publishing, LLC
https://regalhousepublishing.com

For Thomas Cervone & David Friday

Too Certain Even to Long For on Certain Days

My best friend, Keith Gentile, scored me the job at Acme Toy Warehouse, way down the Allegheny River, east of Pittsburgh, in Indianola, PA—wherever the hell that was. Clearly no place. But no place was fine with me.

Keith had flunked out, dropped out—whatever you want to call it—after his first semester in college when he got his girlfriend back home, Bonita Guida, pregnant. Keith's aim had been to save enough money on the pittance he earned at the warehouse, so they could get married, raise the kid, and take it from there. Lodged in his crazy, troubled head was that the pregnancy was all his fault—and maybe it was—that he could fix everything by making himself more miserable.

Bonnie ended up having an abortion. Keith lovingly stuck with her through it all, helped pay for it, even though he wanted her to have the baby. I chipped in too and sat next to Keith at the clinic after Bonnie disappeared behind a windowless locked door. She and Keith stayed together another few weeks, through the unbearable Christmas holidays, in their cruddy garret above a florist on Penn Avenue, right across from The Little Sisters of the Poor; then, when the abortion came to light, they moved back home with their respective sets of brokenhearted parents.

Keith and Bonnie were done. This was obvious to everyone. But Keith couldn't let it go. While the pregnancy had fried him like a hot wire, the abortion torched him with guilt and the darkest recriminations. He shouldn't have had premarital sex—Mortal Sin One. Then the abortion—Mortal Sin Two: the Sixth Commandment that God Himself had etched with his finger into the stone tablet Moses delivered to the Israelites from Mount Sinai—*Thou Shalt Not Kill*.

"There it is, Fritzy," Keith sputtered, misfired and shorted out, his voice like air wheedling out of the pinched neck of a strangled balloon. "Murder." Not to mention the straight shot to hell, no appeals, no parole. Conflagration. Forever.

Before the Warehouse, I hadn't even considered *acme* a real word: "the point at which someone or something is best, perfect, or most successful." I had seen *acme* only in cartoons, so I figured the word was a hundred percent made-up, a ludicrous trochee to accompany the absurd hijinks of Bugs Bunny, Daffy Duck, Elmer Fudd, and company.

The Acme Corporation figured prominently in Road

Runner cartoons. Wile E. Coyote often wielded Acme products—dynamite, and rockets he strapped to himself in attempts to snare Road Runner. His ruses always backfired, literally, leaving him cross-eyed, charred and stupefied—stars orbiting his head—as the loony Road Runner *beep-beeped* and lit out at warp speed. I had always suspected those cartoons were parables of inevitable disaster, cautionary tales, just a few pixels beyond my ken—like the warehouse, a lavish cartoon, swarming with cartoon characters, including Keith and me.

Every morning, with the late summer sun in our faces, the two of us drove to Acme along Allegheny River Boulevard in Keith's green 1966 Plymouth Satellite. It had been the Gentile family car until Keith, too drunk to drive, but too maudlin over Bonnie, too hardheaded, to relinquish the wheel—I had been with him—wrecked it on the ice in front of Tootie's Diner. Mr. Gentile bought a new car with insurance money and had the Satellite, pretty much totaled, fixed—bare minimum, still on the verge of collapse. He then gave it to Keith for back and forth to work, and Keith had to pay back his dad, monthly, for the cost of the repairs.

As we rumbled further upriver into the country, black sunken steel mills gave way to marinas strung with pleasure boats, and the mist lifted off the river. We smoked cigarettes, listened to music and caught a few scores on the radio. The hot songs were "Let's Get It On," by Marvin Gaye, and "Delta Dawn," by Helen Reddy. The Pittsburgh Pirates, in their 92nd season, lurched stricken through the season without Roberto Clemente, who had perished in a plane crash, New Year's Eve, on his way to deliver supplies to earthquake victims in Managua. Some new guy, Richie Zisk, played right field where the grass withered and died.

Through the windshield, it was all out there, the last of the green and gleaming, leaves still clinging to the trees, girls in bikinis sunning on wharves, and there were things we thought we knew—perhaps even a way through all the bullshit. Keith and I had known each other since kindergarten; the silence between us was soothing, completely natural. He was the closest thing to a brother I'd ever had.

I was in-between, straddling an invisible line bisecting ruin and the verge of something important that might shove me out my rut in Pittsburgh; and East Liberty, the neighborhood Keith, Bonnie, and I had grown up in. For a little over a year, I'd been involved with Claire Raffo, a mysterious, brilliant girl exactly my age, also from East Liberty—we had even gone to grade school together at Saints Peter and Paul on Larimer Avenue—and I was clearly in her sway. She attended Pitt and read impenetrable books by Carl Jung and James Joyce and Jorge Luis Borges. Her apartment was perfumed with candles and incense, draped with batik. She didn't shave her legs or under her arms. She called me Frederick, my baptismal name, though I went by Fritz.

At Claire's urging, I had enrolled in a night class—Introduction to Literature—at Community College of Allegheny County. I still lived with my parents, Travis and Rita Sweeney—though I spent many nights at Claire's apartment—a couple of characters right out of Tennessee Williams and Edward Albee. Everyone I knew was crazy, so working in a 30,000 square feet asylum—a colossal steel cube of toys and maniacs—didn't faze me at all.

Initially, I found the warehouse a relief. I worked alone in what was dubbed *Salvage*, reassembling fragmented toy sets split apart during shipping. My job was to sort through enormous bins of discards, rejects, and fragments and reunite them according to the manufacturers' packaging contents. On a clipboard, I accounted for each piece I inventoried. The job was pleasant enough, sitting there on the warehouse's cool concrete floor, smoking cigarettes and eating Junior Mints. But it wasn't long before the disembodied limbs and decapitated heads, horses, dogs, cars, dinosaurs, wheels, blocks, cogs and spindles that fit nothing began to freight me with the absurdity of my task: reassembling tiny broken worlds I cared nothing about.

Along the face of Acme were a dozen bays for the tractor-trailers that rolled in and out all day. Freight was delivered, unloaded by hand on to wooden pallets on the dock; then the hard-hatted pickers, piloting forklifts, skewered the pallets on long steel tines and drove them off to store in gray metal racks that stretched, row after row, the length of a football field, six storeys to the silver insulation that packed the ceiling girders. When an order to be filled arrived, a picker delivered the inventory from the racks to the dock, and it was loaded on a truck and hauled to its destination. That was it, Acme's *raison d'etre*, day upon day: indistinguishable products—ever diminished, ever replenished—rolled in, rolled out.

The warehouse boss was a guy named Danny, a fashion-hippy, who looked like *Abbey Road* John Lennon—shoulder-length hair, bushy brown beard, and circle wire-rims. He wore lavish flowered shirts, the top two buttons undone, revealing a gold necklace in a ferocious nest of hair. He drove a black Pantera, in which he tooled into the Acme lot and parked among the used junkers his employees spilled out of with their lunch buckets.

Danny sold himself as a cool, kind-of-regular guy—

like he understood working stiff warehousemen—always friendly enough with me, like "Hey, man, what's up?" and a practiced smile. But I knew I couldn't trust him, and I knew he knew I didn't give a shit about the job.

After his perfunctory morning stroll through the warehouse, Danny disappeared, via a corkscrew staircase, into his lair, way up above us, the only air-conditioned patch in the entire sweltering building. There he sat all day behind one of those espionage windows from which he could scrutinize the warehouse, like a god in his magic booth, but none of us could see him—the kind of invisible, voyeuristic omniscience I so longed for. Until five straight-up, we never glimpsed him again, and it became easy to forget that there existed any reason to be in that building other than the daily cross of boredom and confinement.

The front-line guys who worked at Acme, the pickers, were lifers. Decent enough—with wives they referred to as *the Mrs., the little lady, the old lady, the ball and chain, the boss.* Kids, houses, the whole deal. Union men: forklift gigs at the warehouse they didn't want to fuck up, already counting off the number of thuds left in the time clock until they could punch out for good and retire.

Keith, a non-Union apprentice picker, and I were

the youngest of them—and another picker, a married guy we hung out with, only a couple years older than us, with two little kids, Arthur Cover. The three of us took our fifteen-minute breaks at ten and three, with the others, in the fly-filled, windowless block room with its fridge and microwave. They kept their head-gear on, grumbled about the Pirates and the Steelers and their fucked-up jobs, bought Funyuns and Fritos and Ho-Hos from the vending machine, chain-smoked, and washed it all down with coffee from fuming thermoses.

They didn't know who I was and they didn't want to know. Keith tried to introduce me. They gave me the once-over, kind of nodded—not unfriendly, merely disinterested, but there was nothing to keep their attention. I was the only one in there without a hard hat. Guys like me came and went.

Keith, Cover, and I never ate lunch in the break room, but rather on the dock, dangling our legs over an open bay, waiting for Munch's Lunch, a giant square truck, stocked with junk, that showed up at noon. I always bought a couple of deviled crabs. We snuck a few tokes from a roach, then killed the last minutes before the horn with cigarettes.

Once or twice a week, during lunch, we drove down Blue Run Road, passed a number on the way, then took a gravel two-track to Sam and Ann's, a crude plank

like he understood working stiff warehousemen—always friendly enough with me, like "Hey, man, what's up?" and a practiced smile. But I knew I couldn't trust him, and I knew he knew I didn't give a shit about the job.

After his perfunctory morning stroll through the warehouse, Danny disappeared, via a corkscrew staircase, into his lair, way up above us, the only air-conditioned patch in the entire sweltering building. There he sat all day behind one of those espionage windows from which he could scrutinize the warehouse, like a god in his magic booth, but none of us could see him—the kind of invisible, voyeuristic omniscience I so longed for. Until five straight-up, we never glimpsed him again, and it became easy to forget that there existed any reason to be in that building other than the daily cross of boredom and confinement.

The front-line guys who worked at Acme, the pickers, were lifers. Decent enough—with wives they referred to as *the Mrs., the little lady, the old lady, the ball and chain, the boss.* Kids, houses, the whole deal. Union men: forklift gigs at the warehouse they didn't want to fuck up, already counting off the number of thuds left in the time clock until they could punch out for good and retire.

Keith, a non-Union apprentice picker, and I were

the youngest of them—and another picker, a married guy we hung out with, only a couple years older than us, with two little kids, Arthur Cover. The three of us took our fifteen-minute breaks at ten and three, with the others, in the fly-filled, windowless block room with its fridge and microwave. They kept their head-gear on, grumbled about the Pirates and the Steelers and their fucked-up jobs, bought Funyuns and Fritos and Ho-Hos from the vending machine, chain-smoked, and washed it all down with coffee from fuming thermoses.

They didn't know who I was and they didn't want to know. Keith tried to introduce me. They gave me the once-over, kind of nodded—not unfriendly, merely disinterested, but there was nothing to keep their attention. I was the only one in there without a hard hat. Guys like me came and went.

Keith, Cover, and I never ate lunch in the break room, but rather on the dock, dangling our legs over an open bay, waiting for Munch's Lunch, a giant square truck, stocked with junk, that showed up at noon. I always bought a couple of deviled crabs. We snuck a few tokes from a roach, then killed the last minutes before the horn with cigarettes.

Once or twice a week, during lunch, we drove down Blue Run Road, passed a number on the way, then took a gravel two-track to Sam and Ann's, a crude plank roadhouse in a forsaken cove, right on the river. We grabbed greasy cheese-steaks and drank beer at a picnic table on the porch. Keith and I were pushing twenty, but the barkeep-cook, a big slab with a ZZ Top beard and Steelers cap, was hardly finicky about underage drinkers.

That was my favorite part of the job—those lunches on Sam and Ann's capsizing back porch, rusted screens ripped and flapping. Dragonflies lit on the edge of our plastic cups and didn't stir as we sipped from them. How good, how clean and right, that cold beer tasted. I let it carry me away as I stared, as long as I could, before shielding my eyes, at the blinding, still, jade Allegheny, suddenly blood-red from the sun, straight-up, falling into it. The river widened there, more a lake or estuary, its opposite bank, seemingly miles away—another country, too far to swim to, too glorious to imagine, too green and blazing to even long for on certain days: the other side, those unnamed, wholly good things Keith and I still hoped for and had sworn to achieve. Not a sound, but for the occasional breach of a massive carp or lap of a played-out wake, that finally fetched us, from an invisible boat. Dreamily, not saying a word to one another, no one else on the porch, we put aside the future, even the next minute on those languid early afternoons. Maybe another day we'd cross over to the far side, the other life—of clarity and rectitude. It would always be there, I assumed. The future.

Then, in an instant, late already, the way it always happened, it was past time to haul ass back to Acme. We jumped in Cover's over-torqued, '65 chartreuse Mustang convertible—each fender gooped with Back Magic, tail-pipe wired to the back bumper, the muffler *rat-a-tat-tatting* like a 50 caliber—and peeled along the gravel as he fishtailed onto Blue Run, showering us in upswelled grit, threw a Mott the Hoople eight-track into the console, dialed *Volume* to the far-right, and floored it until we were back in what passed for the real world. The *cruel world*, as my mother, with that rueful *fuck everything* smirk, liked to call it. I remained in that river trance for maybe another twenty minutes, sorting my little plastic charges, until I grew drowsy and bored—attempting to look busy, a charade much more exhausting than real work—and prayed for the five o'clock whistle.

I had come to look forward to my class at CCAC. My teacher, a brand-new PhD, Dr. Leo Rivera—a Vietnam veteran, supposedly married to a South Vietnamese woman he'd met in-country (though no wedding ring)—had published a book of poems. A poet. Whatever in the world that designation might have meant in a man's life. Claire liked poetry and sometimes read it to me. Her favorite poet was Sylvia Plath. I didn't understand Plath's poems at all. But tapers flared in my head when Claire, under a spell, dark nights in bed, surrounded by candles, read Plath's words—the trembling and awe, the stone transoms quaking, incense furling over the nave, during the Ordinary, the instant Father Guisina rumbled *Kyrie Eleison*. What I *heard* at Mass. What I *heard* when Claire invoked Plath. The body. The blood. All that blood. Plath's haunted, possessed poems scared me—like Claire often scared me: "Or shall I bring you the sound of poisons?" After Claire read that Plath line, she looked up at me and smiled, then kissed me.

Rivera smoked one Lucky Strike after another, in mid-sentence fussing with that shiny, pretty white cigarette packet with the crimson bullseye, snagging another square and firing it up with a chrome Ronson. He had a great wooly head of hair, in which smoke congregated, like webs of funnel spiders in black morning grass. He stalked back and forth across the room, hunched, rumpled, occasionally pausing to gaze very sincerely at us before marching on, talking, puffing. The smell of lighter fluid. The darkening world beyond the classroom windows, autumn coming on. Back and forth. Corduroy jacket, knit necktie, basic button-down shirt, khakis, work boots. Sometimes he took the jacket off, and rolled up his sleeves. He always loosened the tie.

Occasionally, Rivera read us his poems. Of jungles, yes, diabolically green, Tiger shrikes—a delicate sparrow-like bird—wafting on thermals from Gehenna, a lair of boys pledged to murder one another; and the stench of burning shit; rock apes; trench foot. Chu Lai, Bien Hoa, Quang Tri, Danang. How to cool in drums of diesel fuel rusty cans of Schlitz left sitting on a tarmac for months at an abandoned LZ. M-16s and lift-ships. But no blood. No names. He hadn't wanted to know names, nor faces. He delivered these poems almost sheepishly, a tad bemused, seemingly exhausted, an odd distant smile stealing across his lips as he finished and fired up a smoke. He swore he'd have us each write our own poem—which terrified me.

One day, he passed around a hunk of shrapnel: twisted gun-metal gray, rust at the jagged edges, silvery where the school room ceiling lights obscenely caught the declivities and it shimmered to life. Desk to desk, each of us turned it, warily, over and over—as if it might come to life and explode. Rivera said nothing, simply accepted it, in his palm, when the last student had studied it, smiled, and placed it in his desk.

He had a dog named Sean, supposedly after a buddy of Rivera's killed in Vietnam, a smallish, sweetheart brown and white collie-shepherd mix, a mutt, that arrived at varying times after class had begun, but always within the first few minutes—after Rivera was throttling about the room; gesticulating with a Lucky, occasionally slashing something illegible on the board, pausing a half-sec to stare wide-eyed at us and flash his charming smile.

Sean's appearance was an unfailing, scripted ritual. There came scratching and an audible yearning whine. Rivera strode to the door, opened it, and Sean threw himself madly upon Rivera, as if he'd been searching, lovelorn, years and years for him. He chortled and wagged and convulsed, nearly climbing Rivera who embarrassedly shushed, cooed, and petted him until Sean finally settled, stretched out, eyes open, next to Rivera's desk, and never stirred until the session concluded. Then he followed Rivera out the door, and presumably accompanied him home. Rivera never made any excuses for the interruption—he did introduce Sean as his dog, and by name, very shyly, the very first evening he showed up—and simply resumed class after he had calmed down.

I had owned a dog once, for only a few weeks, about six years earlier, the first and only dog my family had ever had. He disappeared one night in a blizzard. He also had arrived in a blizzard. My parents found him, one bitter, boozy 2:15 a.m., waiting for them at the curb outside Foxx's Grille, on their convoluted route home from work. My mother named him Fred, after her father, Federico, who had died when his cobbler shop burned down when she was a kid.

I thought often of Fred, the dog—and my grandfather too, picturing him one of those writhing souls at the stake in Purgatory—and sometimes thought I spied him, skulking around the trash drums in the alley behind Claire's apartment. Claire asked me if I had cried about Fred. I had to ask her which Fred. Then we talked about crying—which she recommended.

I had nothing against crying, but couldn't remember the last time I had, which bothered me, and I tried to dredge up the memory. I wept in dreams, but when I woke, I was calm and dry-eyed, and glad. There's always plenty of crying up ahead.

Claire studied dreams and wrote them down the moment she woke from them—at three and four in the morning. But I wasn't about to turn on a lamp and take notes in the middle of night. My dreams were so crazily memorable, I knew I'd remember every frame of them in the morning. All I remembered, however, was that I'd dreamt. The dream itself had been erased.

Jung believed that dreams were revelatory rather than simply a crazy fractured meta-narrative. They were ways of "integrating our conscious and unconscious lives"—two things I preferred not to mix. My dad often talked about how we're all more than one person, which I did not disbelieve, but finding your route through a single life, much less two, seemed already hopeless. Claire explained Jung's theory of *Individuation*: "the mind's quest for wholeness." This struck me as sound—striving with all of your heart and soul to be a good person instead of an asshole, to be happy instead of unhappy—though not terribly original and easier said than done. And, of course, I didn't know where or how Jung grew up. But the people on Saint Marie Street, where I lived, had their asses kicked so royally every day just trying to get their hair combed and out the door to eat eight hours of shit so they could put milk and bread on the table, and shoes on their kids' feet. *Individuation* was way the fuck down on the list of goals. Self-actualizing was a paycheck and maybe a six-pack, a little peace and quiet on Sunday in front of the Steelers on TV. Shit, they didn't have time to think about how they felt. Start thinking about how you feel, and you'll never get out of bed.

Claire had been after me to take the Myers-Briggs test, and finally I agreed. But I answered *neutral* on each question, and she got a little pissed. She said I had in essence cheated and hadn't taken the test seriously and, by extension, hadn't taken her seriously. Or maybe something was off with me if I regarded everything having equal importance. Or maybe I was a nihilist who just didn't give a shit about anything, and had zero curiosity. Maybe I was just scared, she said, to learn who the hell I was. There was a question on the Myers-Briggs about trying to avoid conflict. That was the only question I answered definitively—because I do try to avoid conflict. Who doesn't? I grew up in East Liberty—just like Claire. Nobody wants trouble, and it's headed your way anyhow. That's how I saw the Myers-Briggs—trouble: a set-up, a sucker game. That's why I opted for *neutral*. Claire said that *neutrality* is synonymous with *indifference*. I didn't disagree.

The first thing Rivera gave us to read was "The Myth of Sisyphus," by Albert Camus. Its first sentence is: "The gods had condemned Sisyphus to ceaselessly rolling a rock to the top of a mountain, whence the stone would fall back of its own weight." All we really know is that Sisyphus offended the gods, trifled with them in some unforgivable way. In high school English, I had picked up through Aeschylus and Sophocles that crossing the gods, who had no sense of humor, was a bonehead play. Camus's essay forwards a number of theories as to why Sisyphus received such imaginative punishment. It's rumored that he was a smart-shit, maybe a thief, cutting shady deals, lying his ass off, playing one god against the other. Real rube capers. I knew guys like him. I also knew "The Myth of Sisyphus" was a parable—one I knew by heart, having heard again and again, from my parents, real-life versions of it. Everyone, at birth, is assigned a rock. The best you can hope for is a smaller one.

The second sentence is: "They had thought with some reason that there is no more dreadful punishment than futile and hopeless labor." I didn't have to pay—actually my parents had paid—to take a class to get that life is a shit-eating enterprise, though I don't want to give the impression that I'm gloomy or bitter, or that I've been alive or employed long enough to have been beaten into disillusionment. Before my post at the warehouse, I had been, respectively, though not contiguously, a night watchman for three months, a busboy for six weeks, a stock boy for two days, a roofer for ten days, and a hod carrier for three weeks. I had quit or been fired—the distinction had blurred to irrelevancy—from each job. Therein was my resume. My threshold for suffering was below sea level.

During class, Rivera paced abstractedly about the room, stabbing at us with an unlit Lucky.

"What are you going to do with your lives?" he

asked. No one answered. "I'm serious. What are you going to do? What kind of rock, what kind of millstone, are you going to dangle life-long from your neck until you're bent in half and your nose is scrolling your one-sentence eulogy in the dirt?"

He stared at us and fired up, took a massive drag and blew a shroud of smoke that hovered the silence.

"C'mon, what are you going to do?"

People testified that they'd be lawyers, nurses, accountants. They had plans. They were getting out.

As if in pain, Sean cried out in his sleep and pawed at his face.

"He's having a bad dream," Rivera said.

The job at the warehouse turned into existential agony. Every day, my pile of orphaned refugees grew: the fireman in search of fire; the mustachioed police chief locked from his jail; the spinster school-marm bereft of pupils and schoolhouse; garrisons of lost knights, gladiators, cowboys, Indians, Marines. Their enameled fortitude mocked me, as I attempted to reconstruct their shattered lives and reunite them with their renegade effects: tiny swords, shields, pistols, purses and hats, teapots and hammers, a ceaseless inventory of the forgotten and misplaced infinitesimal.

For the first two weeks or so, I played it straight. I painstakingly combed through mountains of ephemera to find every cowboy's horse, saddle, hat, and pistol. Same with the rest of the cast of characters. But Travis and Rita had raised me to recognize a fool's errand. Like Sisyphus, I was being punished by the gods. Instead of a rock, they sent at me an unending queue of meaninglessness plastic. The clerk of *nada*, I started to worry about what my life was worth, apart from the $2.10 an hour I earned at the warehouse. In trickles—one by one, initially—I began getting rid of my little charges and their trappings. I slipped them into my pockets, falsified tallies on the clipboard, took them home and stashed them in the garbage can beneath our kitchen sink. During lunch at Sam and Ann's, I drank beer on its rotting, half-submerged dock and hurled little people far out into the river where they bobbed a few minutes, then drowned, while Cover and Keith laughed and egged me on.

I fired until my pockets were empty, my load lightened a tad—at least until I got back to the warehouse. Cover rolled a joint, his long blond hair hanging limp in the heat blasting us in corrugated waves from the river. He wore a T-shirt embossed with Mickey Mouse. Keith drank the rest of the beer straight from the pitcher, and smiled at the thought of a Union card. His signature red bandana pulsed at each throb of his temples. We mooned another moment over the river. Then Cover looked at his watch, sprinted in his ratty tennis shoes on the cuffs of his baggy bells, then we were in his Mustang, roaring toward Blue Run, spitting gravel, laughing—because we were late as hell and a little wasted and what else was there to do but laugh.

Keith made only a few cents per hour more than me, but at least he got to cruise around all day on a forklift and wear a hardhat. His new plan was to join the Union and stay at the warehouse. That would get Bonnie's attention. That kind of vested good money. They'd get back together and raise a family.

Cover was officially an apprentice, almost a Union man, but not quite, in it for the long haul, his bed made: wife and two babies. "Serious shit," he often said about them, though he beamed with happiness any time they came up. Cover and his little family kept Keith and me kind of hopeful. We still dreamed of that better life, vouchsafed in all the lore: a family and house, a solid job and wage you could tolerate without becoming a drunk or blowing your brains out—especially Keith, who wanted Bonnie back, that vanished baby back, to scrub clean that big black stain on his soul.

For the first two weeks or so, I played it straight. I painstakingly combed through mountains of ephemera to find every cowboy's horse, saddle, hat, and pistol. Same with the rest of the cast of characters. But Travis and Rita had raised me to recognize a fool's errand. Like Sisyphus, I was being punished by the gods. Instead of a rock, they sent at me an unending queue of meaninglessness plastic. The clerk of *nada*, I started to worry about what my life was worth, apart from the $2.10 an hour I earned at the warehouse. In trickles—one by one, initially—I began getting rid of my little charges and their trappings. I slipped them into my pockets, falsified tallies on the clipboard, took them home and stashed them in the garbage can beneath our kitchen sink. During lunch at Sam and Ann's, I drank beer on its rotting, half-submerged dock and hurled little people far out into the river where they bobbed a few minutes, then drowned, while Cover and Keith laughed and egged me on.

I fired until my pockets were empty, my load lightened a tad—at least until I got back to the warehouse. Cover rolled a joint, his long blond hair hanging limp in the heat blasting us in corrugated waves from the river. He wore a T-shirt embossed with Mickey Mouse. Keith drank the rest of the beer straight from the pitcher, and smiled at the thought of a Union card. His signature red bandana pulsed at each throb of his temples. We mooned another moment over the river. Then Cover looked at his watch, sprinted in his ratty tennis shoes on the cuffs of his baggy bells, then we were in his Mustang, roaring toward Blue Run, spitting gravel, laughing—because we were late as hell and a little wasted and what else was there to do but laugh.

Keith made only a few cents per hour more than me, but at least he got to cruise around all day on a forklift and wear a hardhat. His new plan was to join the Union and stay at the warehouse. That would get Bonnie's attention. That kind of vested good money. They'd get back together and raise a family.

Cover was officially an apprentice, almost a Union man, but not quite, in it for the long haul, his bed made: wife and two babies. "Serious shit," he often said about them, though he beamed with happiness any time they came up. Cover and his little family kept Keith and me kind of hopeful. We still dreamed of that better life, vouchsafed in all the lore: a family and house, a solid job and wage you could tolerate without becoming a drunk or blowing your brains out—especially Keith, who wanted Bonnie back, that vanished baby back, to scrub clean that big black stain on his soul.

Cover supplemented his Acme salary by fencing kiddie pools, toy train sets, tricycles, this and that, he smuggled out of the warehouse. At the end of the day, Keith and I were responsible for throwing the day's accumulated refuse into the dumpster—the usual crap generated by fifty people, and mountains of cardboard and Styrofoam.

During the workday, Cover nipped into the inventory while he picked and left his heist for Keith and me on one of the floor racks in a back corner of the warehouse. We mangled the contraband boxes some to make them look like discards, then Keith and I toted it all out to the dumpster where they tangled, indistinguishable from the trash. Later that night, Cover returned, pillaged the dumpster for the stuff and turned it into revenue. We did this maybe once a week and, in return, Cover laid a twenty on us, nearly as much as I made in two days after taxes.

Other than rite-of-passage shoplifting, I had never been much of a thief. What Cover, Keith, and I were doing struck me as dangerous, but half-justified as well. By then, I had determined that a bunch of pissed-off grown men in a giant building filled with toys was commentary enough on the decrepit human condition, and I had no loyalty whatsoever to Acme or Danny. I basically had no opinion at all about them. They were mere nuisances that accompanied the job I had come to loathe, a job that clearly signaled my own insignificance in the cosmos.

My attitude mirrored my parents' philosophies. At best, employment's a woeful arrangement, but an essential one: give your bosses a day's work, but don't trust them, and be guarded with your loyalty. I had also come to believe that, because of the absurd work I'd been saddled with, I owed my employer absolutely nothing. I didn't know what I ultimately desired, but it wasn't a Union card. Maybe it was Claire and whatever might come after that. Maybe it was just to be left alone—which happens soon enough to all of us anyhow.

Thus, I began to rationalize my collusion with Keith and Cover as righteous, a way to combat inequity, help out an underpaid buddy in need who was just trying to feed and clothe his little family. Your employer lowballs you, treats you like shit, so you steal from him to redress those wrongs, eke out revenge and respect. Back-pay. Pay-back. More than anything, I loved that extra twenty bucks.

"The Myth of Sisyphus" is a decidedly doleful tale—which I had internalized because reading it coincided with my own "whole being" at the warehouse "exerted toward accomplishing nothing." But it's also a tale of a virtuoso smartass, and I knew plenty of them. I even aspired to be one, but I didn't have the killer instinct or the requisite bitterness or the falling-over-funny improvisational mouth like a meat grinder—talents my mother excelled in. But I knew what was up. I knew I was snared, in trouble. I had unwittingly found myself, according to Camus, *conscious*, not yet anesthetized, like those Union pickers, to how hopeless the whole scene was. Maybe like Cover was too. Even Keith. For the moment, I was just the "futile laborer of the underworld," the "absurd hero" because, like Sisyphus, I understood perfectly what a dumb-ass situation I was in. So, I took some comfort in that. *Consciousness*, right? Maybe I even started romanticizing my misery. The more I read, the more I realized that sometimes it's cool, even attractive, to be tortured. And therein was some humor. The Ace-in-the-Hole sentence in the essay is: "There is no fate that can not be surmounted by scorn." My mother could've written that. "*Jesu Christe*," she'd hiss and smile, "I love the way you twist that knife in me. But maybe, pretty please, just a tiny bit to the left." Then she'd wink.

Claire said "The Myth of Sisyphus" is a Marxist allegory, something she declared about a lot of things. "We're all condemned to push our rock up the hill, then watch it tumble back down, Frederick. Over and over."

"I realize that, Claire."

"We have deep and masochistic attachments to our rocks."

"I understand. I really do. But I object to what I see as a badly flawed system."

"So, change the system."

"At $2.10 an hour, it'll take me a while."

"Get a new job."

I knew she was playing devil's advocate, but I was not in the mood. The truth, of course, was that I did not want a job—at least any that I was qualified for. I experienced a sudden moment of *existential dread*—a term Rivera regularly batted around in class. I contemplated what my life would be like without Claire. Did we love each other? Surely, we did, but we had never said.

She had let her brown hair grow long, past her shoulders. It had come in luxuriant and wavy, cowling her face. Her silver eyes were enormous. She wore a violet, thin-strapped nightgown, and smiled. She had that faraway, fading-away look—that occasionally took her over when she imagined she was possessed and hearing voices. She'd threatened once to enter the convent. She wanted to be a saint. Literally. What did she see in me? Losing her seemed imminent.

We sat in the kitchen. Saturday night. Some of my

clothes were in her closet. I hadn't confided that I was systematically eliminating the warehouse inventory I was paid to account for, or that I was a principle in a ring of petty thieves.

"What's your rock?" I asked.

"You are my rock."

I thought I'd leave it at that *double entendre*, if it indeed was one, and merely smiled back at her. She rose and swept through the apartment; switched off lamps; lit candles as she went; put Gregorian Chant on the turntable; peeled back the bedclothes; slipped, like a shade, naked, out of the gown; and lay in bed.

"What do you want to do, Frederick?" she called to me.

I wondered if she meant, for the moment, or forever. I stabbed out my cigarette—she hated for me to smoke—left the darkened kitchen and joined her in bed.

Next on the syllabus was Camus's first novel, *The Stranger*. Its first two sentences are: "Mother died today. Or, maybe yesterday; I can't be sure." Meursault, the narrator and protagonist, is not only unsure of what day his mom died, but he doesn't know her age; and, when he shows up at the "home" (I took it to be like the "county home") —a place it's suggested he shipped her because it was too expensive and too big a pain-in-the-ass to take care of her at his flat, where she had been living—he refuses the opportunity to have her casket opened so he can glimpse her one last time before she's buried. On the face of things, the guy is a jagoff. The class was united in its condemnation of Meursault: that was some telling, hard shit—that kind of indifference. What cold bastard doesn't want to check out his dead mom? It was the least he could do after ditching her in the pest-house.

As usual, Rivera said little, just strolled cryptically among us, his left hand in his pocket, jangling keys and change, a cigarette between the two first fingers of his right hand. Sometimes he closed his eyes as he walked. Like he knew absolutely everything there was to know about Sisyphus and Meursault, as if he were those two, wrapped in one suffering inscrutable husk, but he wasn't about to confess it.

I never spoke in class—I wasn't sure I belonged—but I wanted to raise my hand and stress that it's really not such a big deal that Meursault isn't preoccupied with the exact day his mother died (Tuesday, Wednesday, whatever), how old she is, or that he refuses the invitation to see her corpse. I wasn't exactly sure how old my own mother was—or my father, for that mat-

clothes were in her closet. I hadn't confided that I was systematically eliminating the warehouse inventory I was paid to account for, or that I was a principle in a ring of petty thieves.

"What's your rock?" I asked.

"You are my rock."

I thought I'd leave it at that *double entendre*, if it indeed was one, and merely smiled back at her. She rose and swept through the apartment; switched off lamps; lit candles as she went; put Gregorian Chant on the turntable; peeled back the bedclothes; slipped, like a shade, naked, out of the gown; and lay in bed.

"What do you want to do, Frederick?" she called to me.

I wondered if she meant, for the moment, or forever. I stabbed out my cigarette—she hated for me to smoke—left the darkened kitchen and joined her in bed.

Next on the syllabus was Camus's first novel, *The Stranger*. Its first two sentences are: "Mother died today. Or, maybe yesterday; I can't be sure." Meursault, the narrator and protagonist, is not only unsure of what day his mom died, but he doesn't know her age; and, when he shows up at the "home" (I took it to be like the "county home") —a place it's suggested he shipped her because it was too expensive and too big a pain-in-the-ass to take care of her at his flat, where she had been living—he refuses the opportunity to have her casket opened so he can glimpse her one last time before she's buried. On the face of things, the guy is a jagoff. The class was united in its condemnation of Meursault: that was some telling, hard shit—that kind of indifference. What cold bastard doesn't want to check out his dead mom? It was the least he could do after ditching her in the pest-house.

As usual, Rivera said little, just strolled cryptically among us, his left hand in his pocket, jangling keys and change, a cigarette between the two first fingers of his right hand. Sometimes he closed his eyes as he walked. Like he knew absolutely everything there was to know about Sisyphus and Meursault, as if he were those two, wrapped in one suffering inscrutable husk, but he wasn't about to confess it.

I never spoke in class—I wasn't sure I belonged—but I wanted to raise my hand and stress that it's really not such a big deal that Meursault isn't preoccupied with the exact day his mother died (Tuesday, Wednesday, whatever), how old she is, or that he refuses the invitation to see her corpse. I wasn't exactly sure how old my own mother was—or my father, for that matter. Preferring not to look at his mom's corpse seemed entirely logical.

And, yes, Meursault did remand his mom to the "home," but Camus leaks nothing about the mother-son relationship, nor how being sent off affected Mrs. Meursault. We do learn, once Meursault arrives at the home for the funeral, that she is pretty popular among the other residents. So maybe the home is a way better place for her than living in the flat with her indifferent son. I really couldn't say.

My parents were years from old age and whatever misfire or catastrophe that would render them feeble, forgetful, and assign them, prior to the inevitable, to death's antechamber. I envisioned their senescence: the molten iron left on the ironing board face down, the kettle melting on the eye, my mother—still bleaching her now-white hair blond—half-blind with cataracts and a pint of Four Roses, whipping the Impala up glassy Highland Avenue through sleet—my ever-placid dad, stone-deaf, at shotgun, humming *Que Cera Cera*, smiling, thinking: *I always knew it would end like this.*

Or maybe it would be slow, excruciating: the dozing clock, mumbling TV, a skirmish of medicine bottles on the dresser, baby steps into shadow, *bye-bye*—down the long ivory corridor, through the front door to catch the last trolley to the end of the line.

As an only child, responsibility for them would fall to me. What would I do? Have them live with me and my family? If ever I scored my own home and family. On every street in East Liberty were ancient Italian people, *Nonno* and *Nonna*—they couldn't speak English—biding their time, petrifying, on their children's porches, too weak after years on the glider to even lift their hands when we waved.

I kept my mouth shut during all the commentary indicting Meursault. We were just a few pages into the novel, and I found myself his doppelgänger. "The Myth of Sisyphus" and my stint at the warehouse had done a little number on me. But it had also opened my eyes to my affliction, and I suddenly knew its name: *ennui*, a blood-born pathogen, a contagion, that so many in East Liberty were infected with. Very deeply, intuitively, I had known, all along, exactly what *ennui* was, before I even had a word for it. I had felt it all my life, even before I was born. I was it. The son of it—and I suppose I had my father, Travis Sweeney, a lovely man, smart as hell, a card-carrying agent of *ennui*, to thank for it. My dad tended to want no part of anything, except my mother and me and our tiny orbit. He was okay with very few connections. Yet he seemed very well-connected, a faithful friend with no expectations.

Ennui. Rivera habitually threw the term around.

It impersonates boredom, yes, but so much more exquisite and poetic, tragically seductive, a romantic world-weariness even though, perhaps, as in my case, you'd not yet experienced much more than the precincts of your schoolyard and kitchen. Immobilization and indifference are key symptoms, a sense of futility, the acknowledgement that nothing matters and what if it did. *Ennui*. Trudging ahead—like Sisyphus—even though you don't give a fuck and you entertain not the least hope of succeeding. *Ennui*. It sounded like East Liberty. Even rhymed with it.

I didn't necessarily like Meursault, but I didn't dislike him either. He was someone who dropped into my life for 154 pages in my Vintage Paperback, with its oddly discomfiting cover design—a tribunal of vexed, clerical faces, very much like the faces of my little Acme people, which I presumed were meant to represent the jury that Meursault ultimately faces. My jury of little people.

Meursault is agreeable enough. Like most of us, he just wants to be left alone and, again, like most of us, and, really, through the most convoluted of circumstances—*Fate*, right?—he lands in a jackpot. He has a nowhere job he's indifferent to, but it pays the bills. Sometimes he eats standing at the stove. He becomes friendly with Raymond, the pimp—never a good idea. He suffers a kind of chronic amnesia or maybe he discards each moment after he lives it. He remembers nothing, is essentially without sentiment, though he's solicitous to the old man, Salamano, and his mangy dog.

Then there's Meursault's girl, Marie. He notices at every turn how pretty she is, what she wears, how sexy she is. When she asks him if he loves her, he responds that he supposes he doesn't—clearly a stupid thing to say. Inept. But he's a different kind of guy. I had seen his pedigree around the neighborhood. His tragic flaw is honesty. It does not occur to him to lie, that telling the truth might hurt someone's feelings or get him in enormous trouble. He embodies a decided child-like innocence—like kids at Saints Peter and Paul who told the nuns the truth, instead of lying, and were then jacked up and left writhing on the hardwood. One girl, beaten to her knees on the marble stairs to the chapel, because she admitted she was chewing gum, suffered a seizure. I knew from birth, that if you wanted to be spared one ass-kicking after another, you lied. When asked *Did you do that?* there was only one answer.

The more I contemplated my rock and absurd life at the warehouse, and the more I internalized and exulted *ennui*, the more I resented my job. The pickers, mounted in their forklifts, habitually glided by me, spread out on the floor, in *Salvage*, with my clipboards and packing contents. They smiled—like *What an asshole!*

I renounced the job, deluding myself, but not much, that renouncement was a righteous action, that I had sucker-punched capitalism. The real story, of course, is that I couldn't bear the boredom, the utter stupidity. I developed a daily ruse. I hung out in *Salvage* every day, just long enough to pass the time with Danny on his morning beat through the warehouse. Then Keith swung by on his forklift and hydraulicked me up to my hideout, in the upper racks, of boxes filled with dolls that talked and wet themselves. There I spent the day, other than lunch, reading, napping, killing time. It was easy enough to falsify my *Salvage* reports—which is what I had been doing all along. No one would ever look at them anyway, and I was steadily disposing of the tiny minions. Eventually, I'd be found out and fired, but so what?

Rivera had assigned our first paper: a reflection on Meursault—the ways in which we identified with him, as well as aspects of his character that we found attractive, relatable, flawed, even repugnant. "If you get stuck," he advised, "write about your rock." I thought I had some things to say; but, more than anything, I wanted to impress Rivera. I wanted him to think I was not just smart, but brilliant. I wanted to please Claire too. I worried that she'd eventually leave me because I just wasn't enough.

It was hot as hell up in the fourth tier, near-flush against the silver insulation that packed the naked girders of the warehouse. I lay on my stomach or crouched, my head a foot from the glistering silver Microlite duct wrap, and sweated in my book and over the pages until *ennui* put me to sleep. Keith and Cover occasionally beamed up and massacred me with the latest advanced water pistols. Sometimes we got high up there. The other pickers were hep to my infantile ruse, but they didn't give a shit. They didn't even know my name. I needed to quit. My goofing off would get back to Danny—if he even cared. I figured I'd wait it out, one day at a time. I rationalized that, for all the confusion I felt, I had a paycheck coming—if, for nothing else, my *ennui*.

The weather in the *The Stranger* is unimaginably torrid—Algiers, North Africa—and Meursault is consistently disoriented by it: often drowsy, craving sleep, to simply be relieved of consciousness, anesthetized. The never-ending glare, the abominable heat, "like a furnace," is a theme, a *trope*, as Rivera termed it, that exerts itself in the service of Meursault's discomfort. But this arch case of discomfort—which Rivera explained we all have—is also a symptom of Meursault's apathy, indifference. For instance, Meursault believes that "to stay or make a move came to the same thing." Again, he's not a bad guy, per se; he just doesn't give a shit. Totally indifferent. An East Liberty archetype—a kind of trope in itself. People who just want to be left alone, don't care what they do for a living, don't want to make a mark or stand out: get on the bus at eight in the morning and get off it at six in the evening, just punch in and punch out, do whatever inane thing you're told to do for eight hours, go home, eat, maybe standing up, then watch television, drink beer, and smoke cigarettes until you pass out—and not be fucked with whatsoever by anything or anyone outside the borders of that script. Sometimes, there are wives and kids, maybe church. But there's no plan; in all likelihood, no God. You plant a foot on the earth, then another, hopefully another and proceed in mindless, apathetic fashion. No guarantees. Like Sisyphus. All you can do is hope for a little rock.

Meursault famously murders the Arab, and for no reason at that, other than at Raymond's behest, Raymond the pimp, the batterer, the truly bad egg in the novel. Four pages before he kills the guy referred to solely as the "Arab"—"objectified," as Rivera put it—Meursault observes, about the gun, the eventual murder weapon, that "one might fire or not fire and it would absolutely come to the same thing." The sun and heat make Meursault crazy. He likens it to the same heat he felt at his mother's funeral. The Arab pulls a knife. "[C]ymbals of sun [clash] on [Meursault's] skull," and then he has what amounts to a vision—terrifying, Biblical: "The "sky [cracks] in two...and a great sheet of flame [pours] down through the rift." Meursault freaks and shoots the Arab, then pumps four more rounds into his dead body.

Somebody in class remarked that Meursault was crazy. Period. End of story. The only explanation for what he'd done. He hadn't known the Arab, he had no motive, he was in no danger, it was broad daylight, and plenty of witnesses. Only a madman would give in to such impulse.

Rivera whipped out a Lucky. Sean's tawny flanks rose and fell, his breathing perfectly iambic.

"I don't know," Rivera said, running his thumb over the Ronson's flywheel until a blue flame swayed. He held it there a moment, the unlit Lucky stubbing out of his beard. He finally lit the cigarette. We smelled the singed hair around his mouth, and he looked like he was somewhere else, maybe on that beach in Algiers, playing out that murder over and over, maybe in Vietnam. Then he snapped the lighter shut with the finality of a coffin, and walked across the room, chuffing smoke at the ceiling. "I don't know," he said again. "I worry when inexplicable behavior is explained away, completely oversimplified, completely stripped of its improvisational integrity, as simply *crazy*. Once insanity is admitted to the equation, the story loses its mystery. It's deeper than *crazy*, folks. There's way more than *crazy* at play. It's humanity. It's me and you. And there's nothing crazier."

We talked about that: what was going on with Meursault. My whole life I'd lived among crazy people. *Crazy* was a word of such stamina, pitch, and range. Not merely synonymous with insane, but also *imaginative, breathtaking*. You might be crazy over someone. There were crazy houses—like Mayview and Woodville—where you sometimes had to go. *Crazy* meant nothing. It meant everything. I'd always used it as my default for almost everything, including my crazy parents, but they weren't crazy at all. Like Meursault, they had assumed their roles as strangers according to the cards they had drawn. I'd say to Keith about my parents, and he'd say to me, about his, "They're crazy." And there it is. But what an empty-headed assessment of the unimaginably grotesque complexities of their lives—not even to mention they'd inherited two centuries of silence, and the poverty and shit-eating they grew up with during the Depression and the War—and my mother's pathological *Italianita*, the capital *I* she was branded with at birth, the spine she twirled on. And my dad, who knows, maybe more a mystery than my mother; but, thank God, placid as Buddha, but also like Meursault, like Camus, maybe even Jesus: not a 100 percent clear that anything matters. Everybody was crazy—holding in the stories about where they came from and who they really were?

Occasionally, after work, Keith, Cover, and I cruised by Sam and Ann's, drank on the dock, and threw barbeque potato chips to the carp, big as medicine balls, that breached obscenely, their mouths long tunnels into the Allegheny's prehistoric past.

On evenings I didn't have to be at CCAC for class, we sometimes visited a spot Cover knew, where a concrete abutment from an old barge lock shelved out on the river. We climbed the ladder of rusty rebar jutting out of it and leapt. The water was warm, not terribly deep, but over my head, a swirling fungal green. We swam naked, but kept our tennis shoes on. Tetanus stabbed out of the lethal world below.

A forgotten Quaker graveyard spread the hill above us. In heavy rain, a wooden coffin occasionally worked its way to daylight and sledded into the river. The riverbank itself, spookily shaded by sumac sleeved in webworms, was another graveyard: abandoned cars, appliances, drive shafts and axles, grease pools, ditched clothing, beggar lice, shale and burdock,

My mother rarely cautioned me the way mothers dole advice to keep their children alive, but she passionately warned against swimming in the vast diseased river, biding to swallow the likes of me. And that would be it: she snapped her fingers—signaling my erasure—they'd drag the river for me—and took a puff from her Chesterfield. My father, puffing a Chesterfield as well, flashed his bemused smile and said nothing. She was an accomplished swimmer, had been a star, class of '37, at Peabody High, which she lorded above my father and me. Neither of us could swim.

Keith and Cover were good swimmers. They stroked out well beyond the shore, and floated on their backs. I imagined just beneath my dangling legs a submerged village of the drowned, sorry venialists, building indeterminate sentences in Purgatory, their bone-white fingers grasping at my black All-Stars. It was always then that I finally hit bottom: the eternal sluice of muck, its asphyxiating *squish*, as I sunk, those hands, gurgling whispers: *C'mere. It's okay. We've been waiting for you.*

I panicked, and clutched for the surface, but the river sucked at me; there was no ballast from which to propel upwards as I sunk deeper into the sump. The light from above, a foot, maybe two, above my head, played off the river's face. I made the mistake of opening my eyes and there they were: the suicides and murdered, the simply unlucky and unprotected, the Quaker dead. Running out of air, I thrashed and bucked and swallowed poison water, then cracked, coughing, heaving, through the veil of the Allegheny—and there were Keith and Cover, on the bank, laughing like mad at me, and smoking a joint. Pretty boats motored by in silver spumes. I laughed too and joined them in the mud.

One Friday evening, after swimming, reeking of sulfur and weed, Keith and I, in the Satellite, followed Cover to his house—a clapboard, two-story shotgun rental out in the country, surrounded by woods, wildflowers, leaning cedar stobs strung with rusted barb wire, recently threshed spermy meadows, ricks of split locust, and a lone hoary apple tree, heavy with scarlet heirloom fruit.

His beaming wife, Hally, barefoot—blond and blue-eyed, of course—in a loose apricot dress, met us on the porch that stretched the front of the house. In a blue cloth sling around her neck nursed the baby boy, Kent, who at intervals popped out his blond bristly head, like a kangaroo in a pouch, to study us with his blue eyes. Hally held by the hand three-year-old Star, in a green dress her mother had made—green eyes like Cover, also blond—until the girl could not bear it another second and ran to greet Cover as he walked toward the porch where an old golden retriever, Abel, and a black cat, Ethiopia, lounged.

He scooped her up, covered her with kisses, and proclaimed, "This is Fritz and Keith, baby, my friends from work."

Hally was in the yard by then. She hugged and kissed Cover. Still holding Star, arm around his wife, he kissed the baby's head; and the four of them, in the yard of their vintage house, the descending sun perched on the brick chimney rising from a silver tin roof, formed a tableau of such aching perfection that nightingales and hermit thrushes broke into their evening serenade, a rendition of "Our House," by Crosby, Stills, Nash & Young, I swear, and I worried that this would all be too much for Keith, who tried to smile, though grimaced, the way he did to keep from turning to shrapnel.

Then Hally hugged Keith and me. I reckoned the pulsing of Kent's lifeblood against me, smelled his mama's tied-back long hair, felt a tad faint myself—and then Hally said, "Welcome. I am so pleased to meet you both, and I insist you stay for supper."

We followed the family into the house and took seats on thrift chairs at a thrift table in a room with colossal windows, century-old panes, adorned with tie-dyed curtains. The entire room—the entire house—exploded in light. Star's drawings, macramé hangings, candles spilling colored wax into saucers, plaintive music of Gaelic Monks. Hally and Keith—children depended from them, though they didn't seem to notice—set chipped platters and tureens upon the table: yellow squash, zucchini, tomatoes, potatoes, kale, all fresh from their garden. They ate no meat, but kept chickens for eggs, a cow for milk, goats for cheese. Hally had baked the bread and churned the blackberry ice cream—from their blackberry canes—for dessert.

No indoor plumbing. They drew all their water from a cistern. No electricity. They heated and cooked with wood. They hoped to eventually buy the house, fix it up, little by little, plumb and wire it, figure in some solar. They aimed to do all the work themselves. Cover's job at Acme would tide them over till they became completely self-sufficient, and by then he'd be a Union man. Nothing but blue sky.

As dusk set in, Hally lit more candles situated in wall sconces; and Cover, whom Hally called Arthur—he called her *sweetheart* and *angel*—they held hands—lit kerosene lanterns, and the children fell asleep—Kent nursing, Star in Cover's lap—while Hally played dulcimer, an instrument I'd never heard of, much less seen, and undid her hair, then disappeared in it.

No reefer nor booze nor mention of it. We drank iced Red Zinger. Cover never whipped out a cigarette, so Keith—who smoked day-long to keep his mouth and hands from sabotaging him—and I refrained as well. Without even discussing it, we knew not to mention Cover's side capers—shit, our capers as well—with the trains and kiddie pools. Keith and I were born knowing to keep our mouths shut.

By the time we departed the Cover house, the moonless cobalt sky spilled with stars. We stood on the porch a minute. Cover and Hally announced that, on certain nights—like this—they spied alien hovercraft. Glorious things happen in the sky when you escape the dank tedium of the city. Coyotes yipped in spectral refrain. I loved thinking about the possibility of another world.

The first thing Keith did when we got to the Satellite was fire up a Newport, take half a dozen deep, sighing drags, as we wobbled up the rutted dirt two-track that was Cover's driveway, before saying: "Jesus Christ, Fritz. That was like going to Mass. That was like forty hours. Ten novenas. Like mainlining communion."

I wondered how in the world to respond—picturing a syringe filled with the Eucharist, that first delirious rush of sanctifying grace—when Keith started crying—which he'd give in to when so moved, and he'd been a flat-out bawling wreck since Bonnie. But this was something different. He smiled as he wept.

"Did you see those two?" he asked. "The way they looked at each other? The kids. The dog and cat. The garden. The apple tree. That was paradise, Fritzy."

I suppose Keith and I had fallen a little in love with Hally, and were surely envious of the life Cover had somehow carved out. He wasn't all that different than us. In fact, he was us, yet he had attracted a woman like Hally, a goddess, who was utterly devoted to him. The way she peered fearlessly into your eyes when she addressed you, amethyst beams of goodness radiating from them. She had connections in Heaven. And, yes, the pretty children and the rest of it.

I had absolutely no desire to farmstead, restore a rickety hundred-year-old house, haul water and chop wood year-round, spend rough winter mornings in a plank privy a thousand frigid paces from my bedclothes. Nevertheless, I was thoroughly seduced by the evening: the wholeness, the well-being, the idyll. The abiding love which I yearned for. All of which seemed a million miles from me, and so radically different from my parents' lives.

Hell, yes, I could live like that, I mused—and, of course, thought of Claire. Maybe living beneath a tin roof would appeal to her. She adored all that organic, homemade back-to-the-land stuff. She talked all the time about simplifying her life, and the nefarious chokehold capitalism, the human bent for meaningless shit, had on us all. Uneducated, not a pot to piss in, living with my parents who didn't have a pot to piss in, I was about to be twenty years old. Still…I couldn't help jonesing for that promised monster hit—after hit after hit—until I was too gone, powerless, eyes rolled back, floating in a warm euphoric amnion of sanctifying grace.

In transports, tears streaking his cheeks, Keith related his plan to win Bonnie back, no matter what—a matter of honor. The evening at Cover's had made it all plain: God had inserted Cover into Keith's life. "Like a miracle, Fritzy," he declared. Inside Keith's head, sprockets and pulleys and armatures whirled and clicked and hammered. He and Bonnie would start all over. He'd borrow his dad's new Oldsmobile, a Ninety-Eight—too many bad memories associated with the Satellite. They'd get dressed up. He'd buy Bonnie a new dress for the occasion—a white dress, like a wedding gown. He'd wear a suit. Dinner at some high-dollar restaurant. Maybe Park Schenley, where my dad was a waiter. Serious swank. Chocolates and a bouquet, a boutonnière for himself—and flowers for Bonnie's mom. After dinner, they'd tool up to Mount

Washington, take in the famous view of Pittsburgh's Golden Triangle. Then—as it is choreographed in film and fable—he'd genuflect and ask Bonnie formally for her hand in marriage, and produce the ring. He'd lay a goddamn diamond on her, seal the pact once and for all. Wouldn't that be more than ample proof that he really meant business?

It was full dark by then, the river to our right, silent, invisible. There. Always there. Omniscient. I said nothing, but I looked at Keith, crying and smoking, as he talked, knowing how difficult it was for him to string together these words. I had nothing hopeful to say. The least I could do was look at him, though I wanted to look out my open window at the river. Even if I couldn't see it. Even if I couldn't swim.

Keith admitted that, of course, he and Bonnie would have to talk about the hard stuff: premarital sex, the abortion, their months apart. He'd take full responsibility for it all, and they could start putting all the hard times behind them. They'd talk to the priest. They'd go to confession. They'd sit down and have a heart-to-heart with their parents. They'd get help figuring it all out. A solid year of engagement, no hanky-panky whatsoever—at least no sex—have a big wedding (I'd be best man), start a family, and replace that lost baby (I'd be the child's godfather).

Keith had hatched the thoroughly half-assed plan of a thirteen-year-old—not to mention that the lone night out with Bonnie he envisioned would cost hundreds of dollars he didn't have. But what he did have, and what I sorely lacked, was faith—perhaps his tragic flaw (Rivera had me thinking about tragic flaws). He was a believer—in God, in all the promises, and especially all the threats. Terrified he was headed for hell because of the abortion, he desperately craved redemption, and there was nothing for that but ritual atonement.

I was no longer sure what I believed. I had fallen away from the church. A few years back, when my parents had still expected me to attend Mass on Sundays, or at least acted as if they did, I simply skipped and bummed around Highland Park—feeding the ducks at the reservoir and smoking cigarettes—until it was time to return home. Sunday was indeed the Sabbath at our house, a kind of ritual celebration of do-nothing and impulse, but only because it was the lone day of the week my parents had off from work. I had seen them in church only on the sacramental occasions of my First Holy Communion and Confirmation.

My mother was haunted by a residual superstitious belief, Catholicism as a last resort, something to crawl back to when all else failed. But she also believed in the evil eye, the *malocchio*; spells; potions; sortilege;

and the East Liberty prognosticator *strega*, Grazziella, whom she consulted regularly. Just like Keith, my mother fiercely believed in comeuppance—that you'd be called upon to answer, in whatever mixed-up vision she had of the next life, for your trespasses. Like God was some stiffed bookie who had your name in his ledger underscored in red and whatever kind of bloody working-over you received, when finally his henchmen kicked down your door, you had coming. More than anything, she believed in vendetta, revenge.

My father was at best an agnostic, perhaps, like Meursault, an atheist. He found God irrelevant. When I graduated from high school and turned eighteen—and my mother started calling me a "a grown man" —the pretense that I, or they, nurtured any kind of spiritual life, or aspirations, fell away entirely. A great relief.

Claire believed in God, but she perhaps believed more passionately, more palpably, in the devil. She studied demon possession, and sometimes thought she was possessed. She consulted Tarot and visited palmists. She conversed with the dead, particularly her grandmother. She wanted to be a nun, be martyred, achieve sainthood. On her living room wall was a photograph of Guru Maharishi Mahesh. She exchanged letters with a holy man in Kentucky. Claire habitually threatened to escape Pittsburgh, and she had already begun that departure, to fade away. I had never thought I could keep her.

Keith and Bonnie hadn't seen each other since winter. Claire had always been tight with Bonnie, but they rarely talked after high school. Claire had headed off to Pitt, and Bonnie settled into a filing job at Don Allen Chevrolet on Baum Boulevard and the life-line she and Keith had so naively scrawled in tandem like a couple of kids with crayons. After the abortion, Claire and Bonnie began spending a good bit of time together. Bonnie, too, was set on leaving Pittsburgh and getting the hell out of the apartment, four rooms above a kosher butcher on Margherita Street, she had grown up in with her parents. Good people, immigrants from Calabria—who would never be able to wake a single day for the rest of their lives without thinking of the unpardonable sin their only daughter, their angelic Bonita, had committed: *fornication*. Bonnie's immortal soul was in peril, and they just didn't know how to shut up about it. They wore that mantle of woe like sackcloth and wept daily. They despised Keith. Anathema. *Diavolo*! They blamed him for ruining their precious baby daughter. Mr. Guida wanted Keith dead, but only after he had suffered a long time.

Keith's mom blamed Bonnie, the *puttana*, for everything. Bonnie had manipulated Keith, pulled the wool over his eyes. Keith was a good boy. Mr. Gentile, who had been around the block, was much more reasonable about it all, but he wasn't about to disagree with his wife on something like this. All four parents had taken the pregnancy very, very hard, and then they lost their minds, truly, over the abortion.

I'd recently seen Bonnie when she had dropped by Claire's. She was friendly enough with me, but guarded. Keith and I were best friends. I had been in the car with her and Keith on the way to the clinic, before the abortion, and then after. *Before* and *After*. The contrast was devastatingly obvious. She had flung wide the door to *After* and would never step back through it into *Before*, where Keith brooded like an abandoned dog, ravenous for something that would never be. What had happened between Keith and Bonnie, the abortion, was *irrevocable*—a word Rivera used often in our discussions. There exists that moment—*before* Meursault pulls the trigger, when all is well, yet within the same instant—*after* he pulls the trigger—a shattering so profound, it eliminates the future. Meursault says, just before he murders the Arab: "It struck me that all I had to do was to turn, walk away, and think no more about it."

Bonnie didn't hate Keith, wanted only the best for him, that sort of thing, but she had already put him behind her, Xd out their childish commingled life-line, and was struggling to do the same with the abortion. She didn't even look like the same person. Barefoot, wearing a long, loose black gauzy dress and dangly opal earrings, she'd cut, close as a boy's, her dyed hair, the yellow of a tired kitchen wall, and let it return to its native black—no make-up whatsoever. She peered at me with searing, mysterious coal-black eyes until I looked away. She was reading the same books as Claire, the ones I'd struggled with and put down. She had applied to colleges for the fall—Slippery Rock and Shippensburg, and one in Ohio, another in Maryland. Her parents had forbidden her to leave, but that Don Allen dowry, pledged initially as a nest-egg for her and Keith, was now hers alone to do with as she pleased. She loved her parents, but if it came to breaking with them, she would. Claire had offered to quarter Bonnie until she left for school. Bonnie was no longer Bonnie. She now went by her middle name, *Isabella*.

I had never mentioned my part in the abortion to Claire. Maybe Isabella had leaked it to her, but it was a subject we avoided. I had started feeling a little freighted by it—maybe because of the way Keith was unraveling. The abortion had been Isabella's choice, not Keith's, not mine. I had just been along for back-up, what any friend might do. What could I have done? I really had no opinion on abortion. It had never occurred to me that it might be a sin.

I still harbored a certain amount of guilt, apart from the abortion, over Bonnie. A year earlier, late in blazing, suffocating August, after Keith had split for college, I had innocently stopped by her house with a bag of eight-tracks Keith had asked me to deliver. I'd gone around back, through the cobblestone alley, where the Guidas had a tiny yard with peppers and tomatoes, a fig tree, and a brick grotto thatching a garish statue of the Madonna. The twin spires of Saints Peter and Paul Church loomed over the neighborhood, each crowned with a cross stationed in the mute silver sky. A mother crow, in black shawl, and a murder of daughters, watched silently from the telephone wire overhead.

Bonnie had been sun-bathing, smoking a cigarette, in a flimsy pink-and-blue-striped bikini. Startled, she bolted up from the chaise lounge, let go of the cigarette, tossed an arm across her breasts, the free hand over her crotch, and stood in the canopy of smog.

She hadn't been doing a blessed thing wrong. In her own backyard. Yet, the way she started, then trembled, as if I'd discovered her at something illicit, taboo. As we faced each other beneath the merciless glare, she looked dead into my eyes, not with disbelief, but recognition, a mysterious reckoning, maybe even relief. We'd been friends since kindergarten. It suddenly didn't seem to matter that I'd spied her like this, that perhaps something irrevocable, ineffable, had occurred between us—a pact, a secret—I really couldn't say—because she threw her hands to her sides, permitting me to study her—stilled and sweating in that carnal light—as long as I liked, as if my uninterrupted gaze—I could not look away—signaled my love for her. Had I flinched or even squinted, I'd risk the entire world disappearing. Nor had I wanted to look away, but to penetrate that scrim that separated me from the life I was destined to choose—the better life, the better me, I nearly glimpsed that afternoon in Bonnie's yard, golden bees buzzing at the clover in the raggedy grass. But then illumination disintegrated and became yet another dismal complication—the fact that I was alone with Bonnie staring at her near naked body like Actaeon moments before his hounds rip him to pieces for accidentally coming upon Artemis as she bathed. Goddamn, if everything wasn't a sin.

In the crevasse of Bonnie's breasts presided, from its chain, the Miraculous Medal, an oval pewter icon of the Blessed Mother, designed and executed by French goldsmith Adrienne Vachette after Mary appeared in Paris to Saint Catherine Laboure in 1830. It represents Mary's role—poor Jesus's mom—as the Queen of

Heaven and Earth. Many Italian women wore them—in devotion, superstition, whatever the difference between the two. Though not my mother. She kept hers knotted with a desiccated sprig of Easter palm to her vanity mirror. I was close enough to Bonnie to make out the serpent crushed beneath Mary's unshod heel, her open arms, light rays streaking from her hands, the part in her long hair, count the dozen stars notched in her nimbus.

Maybe I had loved Bonnie in that moment, and maybe she loved me. I'm tempted to say I wasn't myself, and that would not be a lie—or maybe I was most myself, even perfected, in the most elemental vein, because I was struck dumb by what I can only call an apparition from which I could not look away.

Neither of us spoke. The last thing I had at my disposal was words. Since graduating high school in June, I had worked for a brick contractor, my mother's older brother, Patrick: scaling for two bucks flat an hour rickety, lethal scaffold, wrangling hods of brick and mortar into that same soiled sky I stood beneath that day with Bonnie, utterly convinced that I would fall to my death. In truth, I had not believed I would live through my own unfocused, terrified longing that summer, and had remained unsure what I feared more—death or disgrace.

I had always thought of Bonnie as plain, nondescript, destined for dray and that pig-headed shoulder-to-the-wheel fortitude of the dreamless, but a very good girl, kind and steady, not one to quaver at an endless tangle of same days until her interment at Mount Carmel with the rest of the neighborhood—the perfect girl for Keith.

The world had drawn up around me. The sky was close enough to touch. Bonnie, in but the flimsiest scraps of polyester, flickered in that fragmenting, holographic light. Desperate for something—that was very clear—as was I—she held in a thousand years of woe. If woe is beauty, she was incomparably beautiful, though *beautiful* is often a shabby word for something much more powerful. That power, her yearning—that's what I was snared in. It draped us like the filth and stench from the butcher's garbage barrels. I hadn't thought to say I was sorry for showing up unannounced, or even why I was there. Finally, she yanked on a T-shirt. I felt a fool, lifted the bag of tapes and said: "Keith wanted me to give these to you." She smiled, accepted the bag, invited me inside for something to eat, and took my arm as we tiptoed up the fire escape. She might have been pregnant with Keith's baby even then.

The apartment had a mortuary hush, every blind drawn, the furniture in the darkened parlor draped in alabaster bedsheets, altars of Renaissance icons, statues of hemorrhaging saints, daguerreotypes of lost ancestors gaping amnesiac from behind domed museum glass—the ancestral world of requiem in its death throes. Mr. and Mrs. Guida, Gaetano and Fina, were at their jobs downtown, he as a freight elevator operator at the William Penn Hotel, and she a seamstress at Hughes & Hatcher tailor shop—long bus rides, dangling from a strap, then the trudge home to the supper Bonnie prepared every night.

Once inside, I was disoriented, vertiginous, as if the ancient, rotting 2x12 I tight-roped every day to the next storey of scaffold, with a hundred pounds of mortar on my shoulder, had finally cracked and I had one more beat in midair before my plummet. Not the first time I'd had those spells: the black hood, the bare-chested headsman ascending the platform.

Then I was back, in a chair, Bonnie crouched before me, a glass of water she helped me sip. We kissed. A split-second, less than that, not even long enough to call it a kiss—more an obligatory kindness.

"You need something to eat," she said, as if we hadn't kissed at all.

She scrambled eggs and cheese, lit a cigarette, and watched me eat.

Anxious that her parents would discover us, though

it was way too early for them to be home, we decided to take a stroll up Highland Avenue to the park and a loop around the reservoir. She left to change. I smoked a cigarette, then paced aimlessly into a dark, linoleumed hall, off which darted two bedrooms. In one was Bonnie, without a shirt, wiggling into a pair of jeans. The Miraculous Medal had flipped and, even at a distance, I plainly saw its reverse side imprinted like a tattoo on Bonnie's breast: a cross surmounted by a capital *M*—beneath it, two hearts spouting flame, one trussed in thorns, the other impaled upon a dagger, twelve stars orbiting the ellipsoid.

She turned her back to me and then I glimpsed something that I had completely, inexplicably, forgotten: a scar on her back that fell like a skein of white clothesline from her neck and disappeared at the beltloops of her jeans. When we were in seventh grade, Bonnie had spent most of the year in a body cast after a dangerous surgery to correct a birth defect that had crimped her spine. Sister Saint John of the Cross had taken our entire class to visit her after she'd come home from the hospital. We thronged the bed and prayed, at Sister's behest, like a pack of mendicants at a deranged shrine, laid our homemade cards in Bonnie's bedclothes, and stared at her sarcophagus before signing it. I prayed most fervently that I be delivered from that room. It was clear to me—in the way Sister bowed her head and closed her eyes, how Mrs. Guida wept as she insisted we help ourselves to biscotti from the platter she passed, how Mr. Guida tried not to weep, but in the little cell inside his head, where he blamed himself for everything, just like Keith, he ate razor blades—that Bonnie's next stop was the chancel at Saints Peter and Paul, a white pall draped over her white casket, symbolizing the Baptismal gown she wore a mere dozen years earlier when she was cleansed of Original Sin, welcomed to the Mystical Body, the monstrous organ whipped to dolor from the choir loft.

And Bonnie: she was so ashamed at every bit of it, imprisoned naked inside her tomb, unable to move—except to smile and thank us in her wee voice for coming. Ashamed of her home above the butcher's, its dreadful peeling floral wallpaper and curling linoleum, the stink from the killing floor below that wafted through the ductwork, her pitiful parents and their broken English.

The fury built in Sister, like ascending scarlet on a thermometer: her disdain for the shambling immigrant Guidas, for the dauby gaggle of brats she led. It was all our faults, our most grievous faults, this had befallen Bonnie—dying because of us. From His crucifix above Bonnie's head, writhing Jesus concurred. With a black magic marker, I scrawled *Fritz*, like barbed wire, over

it was way too early for them to be home, we decided to take a stroll up Highland Avenue to the park and a loop around the reservoir. She left to change. I smoked a cigarette, then paced aimlessly into a dark, linoleumed hall, off which darted two bedrooms. In one was Bonnie, without a shirt, wiggling into a pair of jeans. The Miraculous Medal had flipped and, even at a distance, I plainly saw its reverse side imprinted like a tattoo on Bonnie's breast: a cross surmounted by a capital *M*—beneath it, two hearts spouting flame, one trussed in thorns, the other impaled upon a dagger, twelve stars orbiting the ellipsoid.

She turned her back to me and then I glimpsed something that I had completely, inexplicably, forgotten: a scar on her back that fell like a skein of white clothesline from her neck and disappeared at the belt-loops of her jeans. When we were in seventh grade, Bonnie had spent most of the year in a body cast after a dangerous surgery to correct a birth defect that had crimped her spine. Sister Saint John of the Cross had taken our entire class to visit her after she'd come home from the hospital. We thronged the bed and prayed, at Sister's behest, like a pack of mendicants at a deranged shrine, laid our homemade cards in Bonnie's bedclothes, and stared at her sarcophagus before signing it. I prayed most fervently that I be delivered from that room. It was clear to me—in the way Sister bowed her head and closed her eyes, how Mrs. Guida wept as she insisted we help ourselves to biscotti from the platter she passed, how Mr. Guida tried not to weep, but in the little cell inside his head, where he blamed himself for everything, just like Keith, he ate razor blades—that Bonnie's next stop was the chancel at Saints Peter and Paul, a white pall draped over her white casket, symbolizing the Baptismal gown she wore a mere dozen years earlier when she was cleansed of Original Sin, welcomed to the Mystical Body, the monstrous organ whipped to dolor from the choir loft.

And Bonnie: she was so ashamed at every bit of it, imprisoned naked inside her tomb, unable to move—except to smile and thank us in her wee voice for coming. Ashamed of her home above the butcher's, its dreadful peeling floral wallpaper and curling linoleum, the stink from the killing floor below that wafted through the ductwork, her pitiful parents and their broken English.

The fury built in Sister, like ascending scarlet on a thermometer: her disdain for the shambling immigrant Guidas, for the dauby gaggle of brats she led. It was all our faults, our most grievous faults, this had befallen Bonnie—dying because of us. From His crucifix above Bonnie's head, writhing Jesus concurred. With a black magic marker, I scrawled *Fritz*, like barbed wire, over the craggy white plaster, the indelible ink bleeding under my sweaty hand. Sister peevishly inspected our penmanship—she shot me a look—so freaked by the visit to the Guidas, so pissed, she couldn't wait to get us back to the school cloak room so she could scream and maybe beat the shit out of us, just to get it off her chest.

Even then, Bonnie was Keith's betrothed. He hovered at the head of her bed, like a crone, handkerchief in his fist, tears pooled in his bug eyes. In the odd nocturnal light, his thorny hair turned white and he trembled. He lingered as we processed from Bonnie's room. Sister said to Keith, *Mr. Gentile*—twice—then snapped her fingers and Keith tripped after us. Sister took him by the arm—she must have pinched him—because he gasped and tears flooded his face. He turned once more to Bonnie. She seemed asleep, but she only wanted to be alone, invisible. I never thought I'd see her again.

I'm certain Bonnie had never noticed me outside her bedroom door, as she dressed, the day I showed up with the tapes. I backed silently down the hall and retraced my steps out of the house, and down the fire escape. Whatever had happened between us was set aside and left to spoil—what passes for the end of something. Merely silence. There is the kiss we shared. I don't like to think of it—though it brought me back from the abyss—and I hope it never crosses Bonnie's mind. It couldn't have possibly mattered. I'd like to blame it all on the unearthly light. Meursault attempts to explain to the jury that he killed the Arab "because of the sun." But now Bonnie was Isabella and she was going away, and the Miraculous Medal was what I remembered best, rather than her exposed breasts. We shared between us not a kiss, but an abortion—what comes of such kisses. I wondered what my *Before* and *After* moment was, if I were on the edge of something irrevocable, or if I had already crossed that threshold.

Keith and I, on the way back from the beautiful night at Cover's, had almost reached East Liberty. I hadn't said a word as he laid out, in more detail with each iteration, his pathetic strategy for winning back Bonnie. When he glanced at me, I nodded as if in affirmation. There was nothing else I could have done at that particular moment. But, if I was worth a ball bearing, it was my lot alone to confront Keith—Keith the maniac, at the wheel, in jagged relief against the dimly lit streets, the fuse rubbed raw, about to blow—and, whatever it took, ram it through his brick head that there was nothing for it, but to let go of Bonnie.

I had Keith drop me at Claire's. I needed to talk to her about Keith and Bonnie—Keith and Isabella. The night hung dark and sultry. A cluster of moths beat wildly about the porch light next to the front door of the giant old house on Portland Street. I walked into the foyer, and took the double flight of stairs to her heavy aged door on the second floor.

Claire wore a white satin night dress I'd never seen on her, though she'd shown it to me once. It had belonged to her father's mother, Erminia Chiara Raffo, who had perished giving birth in 1920 not terribly far from where Claire stood. Claire's father, Gualtiero (Walt) had named her for his dead mother—Claire for Chiara. He had survived that birth, though his twin had not, and Claire credited that repressed trauma for her father's implacable fury, his hatred of women. Walt Raffo was a landscaper, an earth-turner, a boxy, beefy juggernaut—enormous lips and teeth, a head so big and craggy, he had been the twin that murdered Erminia Chiara, even as she gave him life.

A tyrannical, abusive brute to whom she'd not spoken in months, Claire hated him, yet she venerated her namesake and consorted with her. She read books on how to cross that shadow threshold: *spettri* traipsed among us. I too felt the presence of the dead and had been visited more than once by my own dead namesake, Federico, my mother's father. But every Italian in East Liberty was hounded by the dead and deified and prayed even to those they had hated while on earth. I tried not to think of that other realm—flesh and blood was enough to keep me preoccupied—but it was there, just beyond the curtain. I didn't confide any of this to Claire, nor did I quiz her about her conversations with her grandmother. Her pile of university books, from which she constantly read passages to me—Jung, Freud, Norman O. Brown, Marguerite Duras, Borges, Andre Breton—terrified me. And now I had Camus and Meursault whispering in my head.

Erminia Chiara's night dress was not white at all, but ivory, faded in fabric, as it was in memory—a remnant. It shone like the spidered, translucent skin of the very old. The gown was in fact the shade of Erminia Chiara—too sparse, too tattered and retold to capture what might have happened that February morning she heaved with the twins on Carver Street. How cold it must have been. The midwife: her hot water and rosaries. Or: no midwife, no hot water. Just rosaries and blood—blood that hadn't washed away but merely faded, decorating the hem, just beneath Claire's knees. Primroses. Thorns. A tear slashed through the scooped bodice where the soutache embroidery frayed and dripped. Claire had nothing on beneath it.

"This is the gown I told you about," she said, "the one my grandmother wore the morning she died giving birth. Motherhood, Frederick. Such an exquisite irony."

Claire had lit candles and incense throughout the flat, and placed a bottle of wine on the table next to the bed—a simple mattress, banked with enormous pillows, in a corner of the living room canopied with batik and scarves, wind chimes and bells. Vivaldi's *Four Seasons* played on the phonograph. She laid a lavish kiss on me, full-bore, a tad desperate, just that panel of satin separating her from me. Her mouth tasted of grapes. Took my hand and led me to the bed. Mounted on the wall above it was a photogravure of Ermenia Chiara. Short black hair swept across her forehead; eyes haunted by weeks in steerage across the ferocious Atlantic; three babies clinging to her; mouth, a sealed, chiseled line. A gilt frame, *In Memorari* scrolled in a cluster of oak leaves at its base, immured her. Mute—save for her consort with Claire.

On the table also lay a dead male Luna moth, its soft green linen forewings retracted, hindwings like rocket fire—each wing decorated with a hypnotic eyespot—a rim of purple at its crest, then its large gossamer antennae.

"Isn't he gorgeous?" asked Claire. On the bed was the novel, *The Exorcist*, its jacket purple, prurient. Claire was after me to read it, but I refused. "They live ten days, Frederick."

"That's not a long time."

"That's all the time they need. They're portents: transformation—rebirth. They detect, through their antennae, pheromones released from the female, from a distance of several miles, and set out in quest of her. Mating ensues after midnight and goes on for hours and hours." She snared me in another long kiss. "Such passion. Isn't that the most romantic thing you've ever heard?"

"What happened to him?" I asked.

"He got in the house and Cassiopeia killed him, a single swipe." She smiled sumptuously. "He never knew what hit him."

At the sound of her name, the gigantic Himalayan jumped from the floor into Claire's arms and stared at me.

"I got a letter from Allen today," said Claire.

Allen Compton—one of the vile mutant children East Liberty occasionally spawned—vicious, sociopathic, a murderer. Black leather, pointy cleated shoes, cigarettes, slicked hair, switchblade, zip gun, and roaring muscle car with a Hurst shift. Bennies and Ripple, sidling up to Smack. Cock-strong—couldn't be killed, despite his death wish.

He'd been Claire's steady beau for years—since she was just an anorexic kid—but she'd broken with him after she and I took up. Freeing herself from Compton, however, hadn't been easy. He threatened to kill her. To kill me. He wouldn't let go of Claire—Charles Manson powers—and she and I had lived, the previous summer, in terror that he'd break into the house while we slept.

Fucked up and lusting for violence, one night, he rammed his 442 into a car of Black kids on the Meadow Street Bridge. When the cops arrived, Compton was downshifting that Corvair of kids through the railing and off the bridge, stories and stories, into Negley Run, snaking through the Hollow. The judge had told Compton he could go to jail—or Vietnam, where he could be a different kind of killer.

"He sent this along," Claire said and handed me a photograph of Compton. Bare-chested, hair cropped, in camo pants and combat boots, he smiled warmly, innocently. He'd lost all that baby-fat and even the sneer—those carnal dripping lips—that had made him all the more terrifying. His naked upper body was so pale, blameless, boyish. In the backdrop, far off, rose the chimerical green Southern Highlands, entwined in mist, jungle sizzling, too seductive for anything but death. "He looks great, don't you think? He looks happy."

The last troops had returned home from Vietnam at the end of March, so I wondered where Compton could possibly be at this moment. Was he back in Pittsburgh? In East Liberty? Or still in Vietnam, crueler than ever because he'd finally found hell and loved it even more than he'd imagined?

"He looks good," I said.

"We shouldn't fear him anymore, Frederick. The transformation in him is quite clear."

I still heard Compton's 442 revving at the curb in front of Claire's apartment, his cleats on the stairs leading up to her door, she and I huddled naked beneath the sheets, the sheets he felt he owned, as I wondered how I could protect myself against such an animal. He had once forced a pistol between Claire's lips, had nearly beaten Cassiopeia to death with a curtain rod. I didn't want to get into all this with Claire or why the hell she still had anything to do with him. But I knew Compton would be back and that she and I would be powerless against him. *Transformed*: just a different kind of killer.

She pulled me down on the bed and kissed me. I tasted the wine again, and, also, this time, the unmistakable flavor of opium—like taking a hit and holding it a tick too long. Then I clearly smelled it and spied the pipe, its bowl smeared with a tarry nugget of opiated hashish. I kicked the novel off the bed, and gasped when she removed her mouth from mine. It was already too late.

I was under the influence, the Vivaldi so plaintive and seductive—that platoon of violins threshing, the bows across the strings forming the *crux immissa: What choice do you have?* it wanted to know. *How can you turn from this woman?*

"You and I could have children, Frederick. I'd know what to do." She handed me the pipe. "Take a hit."

Of course, she'd know what to do. She'd gobble them up. She would be a formidably spectacular mother—the archetypal Italian matriarch. I loved her most when I thought of having children with her, even though that would have been tragic.

"No."

"For me, Frederick."

"Uh-uh."

"If you love me, take a hit."

If I loved her. I took the pipe: an ornate green, gold, and black glass dragon, long, serpentine, spikes along its spine, the stem its tail, the bowl its horned head. When I hit it, fire from its eyes reflected in Claire's, and smoke seeped from its mouth and nostrils. It smiled and coiled, as Claire smiled and coiled and pressed the flame to it while I inhaled and held in what should never be held in.

Femme fatale. A term Rivera had introduced me to. But I had reckoned with it all my life: Rita, my mother.

I fixed on Claire's chromium eyes—that prick of glass dragon red fire leaking from them. That smile: she had plans for me. That smile: opium, its revolting medicinal taste, like a gulp of Merthiolate, spiders laying eggs in your septum—then another hit—all the while the ghost of Compton's 442 idling just beyond the sash like small arms fire, rockets, assassination attempts. The Vivaldi was soothing, the last strings of *Autumn*, the final leaves cleaving to the sycamores.

"You're in bed with me," Claire whispered. "Can you hear the river? Listen." That couldn't have been. The river was too far off. She rose and walked to the phonograph and removed the record. "Listen." In the candlelight, her naked body, down to the bone, a female silk moth, beneath Erminia's chrysalid gown, flashed like a photographic negative. "Listen." She stood at the open window.

I sat up, and took a pull straight from the bottle of cold white wine. I heard the river, then the lonely cry of geese. I joined Claire. Cruciform shadows of squawking geese, as they flew above the streetlights, darkened the street.

"Their cries keep them from losing one another," said Claire.

When I arrived home from Claire's, early Sunday afternoon, my parents were at the kitchen table. I stood a few feet away, out in the backyard, and watched through the screen door. They were completely dressed, a shock, since I hadn't even expected them to be out of bed— or, at very best, still trying to wake up, smoking cigarettes, and transitioning from coffee to booze. My dad, in khakis and lavender guayabera, ruffles and scrolled stitching, slipped a pack of Chesterfields from one of his fancy side pockets at the hem, a Zippo from the other, and laid them like a pair of Jacks on the table.

On the face of the pack was a jeweled golden crown. *Chesterfield Cigarettes* looped regally across a pale green scape of what I took to be minarets, a bridge across a river, a gondola with its boatman. I suppose it was Turkey, and the river the Tigris or Euphrates. The Liggett & Myers Tobacco outfit that manufactured Chesterfields in North Carolina claimed, in all caps, that its tobacco was a "balanced blend of the finest aromatic Turkish tobacco and the choicest of several American varieties…"

My mother swept up the Chesterfields, plucked one from the packet and held it the way Myrna Loy brandishes an unlit cigarette in movies. She was in a pink dress she almost never wore, as if its beauty had to be parsed out judiciously. I had loved that dress all my life. Perhaps it was madras, a soft, cloudy, floating pink, three scant pearl buttons at the throat, long sleeves. Like my dad, she was barefoot. Her hair, dyed blond, looked so pretty—blinding silver in the sun. I could barely see her face, except her brown eyes, in that blazing cowl. The kitchen had a way of rendering light in a suspect way, but that day the windows had opened to it with such generosity. Kids played ball in the alley behind me. The bat peeled off the cobblestones each time they dropped it and ran.

My dad scooped up the Zippo and, like a mage, was suddenly on a knee before my mother, in the light, putting flame to her cigarette. The Mills Brothers played on the hi-fi. They hadn't spun on the turntable in a long time.

"What's going on here?" I asked from the yard, then walked into the kitchen. "Should I have knocked?"

"I beg your pardon?" said my mother from her cove of light.

My dad got off his knees. "Hello, Fritz," he said. "Have a seat. I was just about to ask your mother to marry me again."

"I would have accepted," said my mother. "But now you've lost your chance."

I sat in my usual chair and my dad returned to his.

"Why are you two so dolled up?"

"We decided to attend Mass this morning," said my

noon, my parents were at the kitchen table. I stood a few feet away, out in the backyard, and watched through the screen door. They were completely dressed, a shock, since I hadn't even expected them to be out of bed— or, at very best, still trying to wake up, smoking cigarettes, and transitioning from coffee to booze. My dad, in khakis and lavender guayabera, ruffles and scrolled stitching, slipped a pack of Chesterfields from one of his fancy side pockets at the hem, a Zippo from the other, and laid them like a pair of Jacks on the table.

On the face of the pack was a jeweled golden crown. *Chesterfield Cigarettes* looped regally across a pale green scape of what I took to be minarets, a bridge across a river, a gondola with its boatman. I suppose it was Turkey, and the river the Tigris or Euphrates. The Liggett & Myers Tobacco outfit that manufactured Chesterfields in North Carolina claimed, in all caps, that its tobacco was a "balanced blend of the finest aromatic Turkish tobacco and the choicest of several American varieties…"

My mother swept up the Chesterfields, plucked one from the packet and held it the way Myrna Loy brandishes an unlit cigarette in movies. She was in a pink dress she almost never wore, as if its beauty had to be parsed out judiciously. I had loved that dress all my life. Perhaps it was madras, a soft, cloudy, floating pink, three scant pearl buttons at the throat, long sleeves. Like my dad, she was barefoot. Her hair, dyed blond, looked so pretty—blinding silver in the sun. I could barely see her face, except her brown eyes, in that blazing cowl. The kitchen had a way of rendering light in a suspect way, but that day the windows had opened to it with such generosity. Kids played ball in the alley behind me. The bat peeled off the cobblestones each time they dropped it and ran.

My dad scooped up the Zippo and, like a mage, was suddenly on a knee before my mother, in the light, putting flame to her cigarette. The Mills Brothers played on the hi-fi. They hadn't spun on the turntable in a long time.

"What's going on here?" I asked from the yard, then walked into the kitchen. "Should I have knocked?"

"I beg your pardon?" said my mother from her cove of light.

My dad got off his knees. "Hello, Fritz," he said. "Have a seat. I was just about to ask your mother to marry me again."

"I would have accepted," said my mother. "But now you've lost your chance."

I sat in my usual chair and my dad returned to his.

"Why are you two so dolled up?"

"We decided to attend Mass this morning," said my

mother, letting loose a sash of smoke that furled in the light around her. "We've seen the error of our ways, Fritzy, and we've returned to Holy Mother Church."

"I'm glad to hear that, Mom." I snatched a cigarette from the pack and lit it.

"There was a Mass for Cuss, Fritz," said my dad. "Today's the third anniversary of his death."

"It turned out fine," said my mother. "The place didn't burn down or blow up."

"We wanted to be there," said my dad.

"It did look like that son of a bitch, Father Guisina, was about to have a stroke when we barged in and walked down the aisle—just the tiniest bit late."

"As you can see, Fritz, going to church brought back bad memories for your mother."

"That's why I only go once every fifteen years."

My parents had grown up with Cuss in East Liberty—the Depression, the War, not two nickels to rub together, etc. That whole rag. Cuss and my dad waited tables at the Park Schenley—where my dad still worked. Cuss had had the habit of church every Sunday, then he hiked up to the reservoir, did a couple of revolutions, and walked all the way back down Highland to our house on Saint Marie. Sometimes he arrived with a pie or doughnuts. For a few years, not all that long ago, I was convinced he was an alien, from another planet—because of a cock and bull story my parents cooked up: that he was impervious to frigid temperatures that would have killed anyone else, and he subsisted solely on sugar, and other things I was too young to reason through, though he had a supernumerary nipple on one of his arms and a rubbery waffling mouth that collapsed in on itself. He had been in general a kind of freak, misshapen and scarred. He limped and wore exclusively the same white shirt and black trousers, monstrous square black shoes that cinched on the sides—East Liberty's Quasimodo—and the only thing that came out of his mouth were lisped, infantile dirty jokes and phlegmy curdled giggles. He drank too much, but everybody I knew seemed to drink too much. I didn't know where he lived or with whom, or what his real name was. I'd been terribly disappointed when I realized he wasn't an alien.

All I had been taught to see, all I'd been able to see, was the freak, though Cuss gave me silver from his jangling pockets and sometime a buck, and he loved reading to me, and I liked him, but was hesitant to say so. I wasn't curious about him until he died. It was then I discovered that—despite the fact that everyone, especially my mother, who took his death the hardest, treated him like shit and gave him the business day and night—Cuss had been universally loved. He meant everything to my parents, but they never admitted what meant everything to them. He'd fought in the war and been wounded. I was a pall bearer at his funeral. He killed himself.

At the very edge of the table, next to my dad's untouched pristine Sunday *Pittsburgh Press*, was a cohort of the figurines I'd begun hauling home from the warehouse and stashing in the trash beneath the sink.

"What's the scoop here, Fritzy?" my mother asked, through a little smile. "You're a little old for these."

The way she looked at my dad: they'd already had some back and forth about these little creatures. She wanted him to say something. However, the fact that I was in possession of, essentially, toys was not likely to trouble him. But my mother was a little worked up about it, though still on the safe side, however—before her mood shifted and she craved a rumble. It was a pretty day and I wanted it to stay pretty, for the kitchen to stay happy and not get pissed off.

My dad had picked up the front page. *Nixon had appointed Henry Kissinger the 56th Secretary of State. In the photograph, Kissinger's mom held the bible he laid his hand on as he uttered the oath.* My parents hated Nixon. In another year, he'd be out the door because of Watergate.

"Where'd you get those?" I asked.

"They're all over the house."

I was embarrassed, red-handed, a little kid. You couldn't bullshit my parents. My mother, especially, was as clipped as the coroner. I spilled what was up, my sorry ruse at the warehouse—but said nothing about hiding out in the rafters or stealing inventory or lunch at Sam and Ann's. I told them I couldn't stand the rote, the absurdity. I left out Sisyphus, but they were scholars of how the dumb shit scars you and then you pass it all along to your children.

"You're going to get in trouble," my mother said. "It's theft, Fritzy."

"It's not theft."

"What is it then?" she asked.

"I don't know."

"Keith got you the job. You'll end up getting him in trouble."

"Keith's not going to get into any trouble."

"He's already in a peck of it. Look what happened to that kid. What's going on with him and this Guida girl?"

"Nothing's going on with them, Mom. He hasn't seen her in months."

"His poor mother. She's sick about it—the whole thing—and you know exactly what I'm talking about."

My parents liked Keith and my mother and Mrs. Gentile, Theresa, were tight. Women you didn't want to rile because they'd never let it drop. Everything was to the death with those two. Mr. Gentile, Mike, a steelworker, was easygoing like my dad.

"Quit the job," said my dad, from behind the paper.

"Listen to you," snapped my mother. "*Quit. Walk away.* That's bullshit advice, Travis."

"Well," said my dad, still not glancing from the paper, "stepping away from something that makes a mess of you and you make a mess of, and you're making yourself nuts over. That's not bullshit advice."

"What about your job, Travis?" she countered.

"I'm doing what I'm able to do to make a living, Rita. Nothing spectacular, I realize, but it affords me a lifestyle I can tolerate and won't make too terrible a mess of. Not that I'm judging, but what about your career decision?"

My father, during these kinds of interchanges—and we engaged in them often of a Sabbath—held the paper at his chest, reading carefully, it seemed, though just as carefully paid attention to the conversation and contributed to it. He felt protected behind newsprint, though he knew it infuriated my mother. He tended to look up only when addressing me. My mother, boiling over my dad's last crack about her job, fixed her gaze on the newspaper, attempting to incinerate it. She worked as a hostess, whatever that meant, at the Suicide King, a suspect, seedy lounge, in the same block as the toney restaurant in which my dad served Pittsburgh's ruling class. I didn't judge my mother, but I didn't want to know a blessed thing about what she did at the King. This was going to go epically bad and, after my surreal night with Claire, I wanted no part of it. The taste of opium ascended my throat. My dad was barricaded behind the *Press*, wondering just how bloody things would get, how long—days, weeks, a month, even two—it would take to blow over.

I snuffed out my cigarette, stood and gathered up the dozen plastic refugees on the table—blameless, stupid, at my mercy. I hated them—my toys—and I desperately wanted out of that kitchen, and the napalm my mother was about to unleash. I wanted out of East Liberty and Pittsburgh, away from Claire and my parents and everything.

My mother pivoted to me. "Where do you think you're going?" She still looked so pretty, wreathed in that pure light. "Sit down."

Like a child, I sat.

Then she turned full bore on my father, clinging to the paper. "Travis, I'm considering clawing your goddamn eyes out and then setting this house on fire. But if you get on your knees again and beg my forgiveness, I'm sure I can avoid such unladylike behavior."

My dad, still reading about Henry Kissinger and his mother, didn't immediately lower the paper. He had learned that Kissinger's mother, a Jewish refugee, had fled Nazi Germany with little Henry, another child, and her husband in 1940 and settled in Manhattan where she toiled as a cook. Her name was Paula. Typically, my father would have shared this with me. He blamed Kissinger for Vietnam.

Meticulous about not mussing a newspaper, he carefully folded the open page, returned it to the table, turned to my mother, fell to his knees, took one of her hands—they didn't wear wedding rings—and said: "I spoke hastily, Rita. I take back what I said, and I hope you'll find it in your heart to forgive me."

What an exquisite Travis and Rita moment—and suddenly I was glad I hadn't rushed out or I would have missed it. My mother was as unpredictably volatile as a junky. Gambling which way she'd veer was a classic sucker game. No one knew this better than my dad. My mother had been his biggest gamble all along. He and I both sniffed a set-up; but, abject on the linoleum, he was playing the odds as he saw them.

My mother looked down at him. She smiled—which meant nothing but danger in this instance. Then she turned to me.

"Should I forgive your father, Fritz?"

"I wish you would," I said without hesitation.

There was a long pause. The kitchen listened.

"I'm afraid I can't do that," she said, turning back to my father, still on his knees, her hand in his. The light had shifted slightly. A sliver of shadow grazed my mother's face.

"Unless"—she turned back to me. "Unless you promise me you'll follow your father's advice and quit your job."

"Rita," said my dad.

"I want him to quit the job, Travis. I insist. You're right. I hate my job. I wanted more out of life and I want more for our son."

My mother was a genius when it came to fucking with people. With her, it was always *The Lady or the Tiger* or really *The Tiger or the Tiger*. There was no way not to get your ass chewed up by an indignant tiger. When she said she wanted me to quit my job, that might have meant she didn't want me to quit my job. It was a test—designed to snare me and, most of all, a way for her to get the better of my father.

"I'll quit," I said.

"Promise?"

"Yes."

"On the grave of my papa, incinerated Federico, your grandfather and namesake?"

"Jesus Christ, Rita," said my dad. He smiled and shook his head.

"Yes," I said.

"Now get off your knees, Travis, and pour me a drink. I've forgiven you."

"Promise?" he asked.

"Yes?"

"On the grave of your papa, incinerated Federico, Fritz's grandfather and namesake?"

"Yes, you bastard. Absolutely. Now fix me something to drink. But kiss me first."

He towered over her a moment, then bent and kissed her before grabbing a fifth of Old Granddad from the cabinet.

"You don't have to quit your job, Fritz," he said.

"Fritz can do whatever the hell he'd like," said my mother. "By the way, I received Communion this morning. I'm in a state of sanctifying grace."

I looked at my father.

"It's true," he said.

She lit a Chesterfield. Smoke wove nests in her hair. Blinding baby sunbirds sang in them.

One evening, Sean did not show up for class. We just figured he was a little late, merely detained by the balmy Indian summer evening. When it was well past the time he should have arrived, Rivera walked to the door, opened it, and stepped into the hall.

He returned with a quizzical look and we resumed our discussion. Meursault has been arrested for his ghastly inexplicable murder of the Arab, and he remains characteristically unconcerned. Nothing seems to bother him and he even forgets for a moment about the murder. He is probed about his seeming indifference to his mother's death, and it's clear the prosecution will seek to defame him and build its case on this symbolic matricide, though they have the goods on Meursault: he pointlessly gunned down the Arab, then shot him, as he lay there, an additional four times, in front of witnesses. The temperature in the magistrate's office is fiery; flies light on Meursault's cheeks. The magistrate, like an exorcist, whips out a crucifix, shoves it in Meursault's face, exhorts him to repent, and asks Meursault if he believes in God. Meursault replies with a simple *No*. Meursault again mentions how hot the office is, hotter and hotter. The magistrate dismisses him, but not before addressing him as "'Mr. Antichrist.'"

Next class, no Sean, Rivera clearly agitated. Meursault is sent to prison. Insects crawl across his face. Marie arrives, for her one and only visit, in a striped dress. Meursault is fascinated by "[its] silky texture." He finds her "very pretty," but for some reason is unable to confide this to her. She assures him that everything will be all right. He'll be out in no time, and they'll resume their romance. They'll get married. They'll bathe in the sea. He is eventually led back to his cell. Marie blows him a kiss, her face against the bars.

"Has anyone seen Sean?" asked Rivera.

I couldn't pin down a topic for my paper and the deadline loomed. Rivera advised us to trust our instincts, when it came to literature, so that's what I elected to do—kind of free associate, assess Meursault like I might someone from the neighborhood, just another freak stalled in the daily grind—the *absurd*, the fact that everything is pointless. You do *this* or you do *that* and it's all the same because you're going to die. So, what's the point? And then *what* after you die? Heaven? Hell? Purgatory? Absolutely nothing? All that really keeps us in check are consequences, right? Extortion. Doing exactly what you're told because there's a nun salivating at the thought of beating the living angels out of you with a board if you don't obey her. Let's say you murder someone for no reason at all, à la Meursault—cold-blooded murder—but, unlike Meursault, you get away with it. The cops are unable to finger you and you're never made to answer on this earth. No prison time. No punishment. No nothing. Total impunity.

But what happens after you depart this earth? Omnipotent God the Father has the goods on you. His scribes have been taking forensically precise notes. He has films. Tapes. Murder's a mortal sin, and if your ass expires with that unredressed capital-crime-sin on your soul, it's a one-way ticket to hell and everlasting agony. No probation. No parole. No cooking off some of your time with an indeterminant jolt in purgatory. So, if you're a believer—and I was—even if you outrun the cops, you can't outrun God because the second you croak, there He is, the blinding light, the Sistine Chapel John Law, floating there with your rap sheet, and a host of strapped-down archangels, in full riot gear, for backup.

Perhaps not believing in God comes in handy, but that involves a good bit of hubris, as in the case of Sisyphus, and you're also playing Russian roulette, like Meursault who is as innocent of right and wrong as a sociopath, and hopes for "howls of execration," when he steps up to the guillotine, so that in his final half-second, he'll get the picture. Maybe God exists; maybe He doesn't. Maybe there's a cartridge in the chamber; maybe there isn't. The muzzle's at your temple. My entire life had taught me to play it safe: twelve years of Catholic indoctrination, and a platoon of homicidal nuns, that absolutely insisted there is a God, and He always has you locked in His stereopticon. So is *goodness* intrinsic or simply the product of fear? Do we have souls?

Rivera waxed about this *other life*, the enlightened better life, out there somewhere, that we were to seek, like mendicants—certainly the life I craved, but had no idea how to achieve; and how, really, is it accessed? That other shimmering life, the hidden one, seemed like those movies where a character removes, by happenstance, a certain charmed book in a haunted Victorian library, and suddenly that panel of books opens to reveal that other life, the better life, a parallel shadow universe that had been there all along, mere inches away, yet totally inaccessible. But which book?

Meursault has no imagination, no yearning. He's unable to picture himself beyond the moment. He doesn't get too riled up about anything. The only turn that really seems to trouble him is that he's not allowed to smoke in prison. Rivera tried to get us to care about our futures, to dream, but in Camus's economy, there is no future—not for Meursault, not for Sisyphus. The only dream Sisyphus chases is his rock.

My father, in his blithe, yet deterministic, decision to not chase a dream, the better life, some superior goal established by forces beyond him, still cared. My mother was just too pigheaded, too perverse, to allow anyone to think she cared. Keith cared desperately, but he didn't have a future. I saw its absence in him during lunches on the dock at Sam and Ann's—the way that sun shredded him, and he turned translucent as if fading away. Cover had certainly given the appearance of a future, and a gleaming one: Hally and the kids and the house in the country, getting *back to the garden* and all that.

I was on the verge of a future, maybe. I sensed it lurking out there, just beyond my grasp, and I hoped I'd brush against the secret panel or reach for the magic book on the shelf—like hitting the jackpot in Chuck-a-Luck at the church bazaar or catching the ace you'd been praying for, down and dirty, on that last hole card. But was I meant for something better? The warehouse was the universe's cruel joke on me: I was ferociously pissed at and obsessed with a constantly replenished mob of one-inch, half-ounce plastic people. And Claire? How did my future and hers intertwine? Was that just another game of Russian roulette?

What rocks, Rivera wanted to know, did we push interminably uphill only to have them roll down on us again? *Regret? Anger? Fear?* We needed to be more vulnerable, he said, but I already felt so damned vulnerable.

Memory is the rock we bully up the hill—not just with our shoulders, but our lips, teeth, and tongue against it. We adore our version of the truth. We make love to it. Over time, we craft it so meticulously that it becomes truth's identical twin, a ventriloquist's dummy that exults and exonerates us while indicting those who have wronged us. We invent what really happened and, because of that invention, what really happened no longer exists. Thus, our ceaseless, futile labor is to exert every waking moment sustaining a fiction, contravening gravity, shoving it uphill, the entire time muttering to ourselves how those bastards ruined our lives, and how perfect it would have all been had they not sabotaged us with cruelty and misunderstanding. We revisit for all eternity the bitterness and resentment that has become our lives.

My mother's true genius, her gift and curse, was that, despite all the unkindness and misfortune that had been visited upon her by others—*the bastards, the son of a bitches, the cruel world*—she had ultimately spited them, spited God and all else—because she just didn't give a shit. Piss on them; they could kiss her ass. In her brainpan played, in agonizing detail, without interruption, the technicolor scenes of ignominy and insult and insensitivity that had forced upon her that Cadillac-sized rock she cussed up an incline steep and pocked as Cemetery Hill, on the edge of Mount Carmel, the *campo santo*, way out at the car barn, at the end of Lincoln Avenue, where the streetcars expired, and their passengers evanesced, that last cobblestone climb past the churches and the military school, the mortuaries—organ dirges grunting out from each of them.

Memory: in my mother's lexicon, a synonym for vendetta. Her gypsy mother, Ouma, my grandmother, exquisitely educated in European convents from where: *France? Morocco? Syria?* Who was too exotically beautiful, a kind of conjure woman, dressed in the clothes of her dead husband, my mother's father, Federico the cobbler, my namesake, who had mysteriously gone up in flames, in his shop, when my mother was nine years old, and she had been there with him the day it occurred. She'd not been able to save him—yet how had she escaped? She had it in her head that she had killed him, though how could that have been? It had been a rat-gnawed wire in the moldy joists, not arson, not murder. *Was that true? Was any of it true?* She hadn't watched demonically as he writhed in flames. *Had she?* But with my mother, everything was arson, murder, slander, blame, culpability. The feud she breast-fed like an infant with the brother she loathed and adored, my uncle Patrick, and how he figured into that shame, and hadn't he been there in the shop the afternoon of her father's immolation?

What she did for a wage at the Suicide King. Was

she a hostess or a stripper?

Now she wasn't able to get pregnant, punished by God for everything she had done and everything done to her, and what she had witnessed and forgotten, and was told to forget, and thus, in her willed amnesiac fog, she invented her rock. The Depression: blood soup, trickling polenta, the sheer shame of her naked body— the *shame shame shame* and glory of her body in that inch of bath water permitted by her mother in the haunted cellar where a man—*Who was that man?*—had hanged himself from the rafters. He still turned in her heart— left, then right, the exaggerated grimace of a Sicilian opera puppet, fine leather boots, limp, anxious hands.

Her eruptive complexion, bad teeth, Roman nose, bleached hair. The fact that my blithe brilliant father, whom she thrived on disparaging as a "gutless wonder," was a waiter instead of a banker or lawyer; that I wasn't attending Pitt or Duquesne. So up—by dint of *Kiss my ass, Piss on all of them*, as she relived, chapter and verse, a past that may or may not have happened—scraped the rock, her daily rite, her cheek against it. By the time she and the rock fetched the summit, she'd exonerated herself (memory as self-exculpation), convinced that even God concurred with her assessment of the cruel world and the fact that its bastard citizens had subverted every minute of her life. There was nothing at that altitude but blue sky and amnesiac ether, the ecstasy of the junky's first sacramental rush. In that split-second, she smiled.

But lies, even truth, are heavy, exhaustingly ponderous. At the very instant that wry smile creased my mother's sweating, turbulent face, the rock trembled. and quaked back down the hill. Sullenly, she chased it, as she must forever, resolved to construct an even sturdier fable about what really might have happened, then drive it, yet again, *ad infinitum*, up its cherished hill. We go on because we must go on, subsisting on falsehood the way we do mother's milk. The truth, what little we can ever know of it, remains horrifying. Your best hope, again, is that your rock is of manageable size. And remember: "There is no fate that cannot be surmounted by scorn."

That was the draft I came up with, mere notes really, but not in those words—words I did not possess. I almost shared it with Claire, but I couldn't bear her critique. I ripped it up and pitched it in the warehouse dumpster with the rest of the trash. Instead, I turned in to Rivera a poem, if it even was a poem, titled, "You're Going to Drive Me to Mayview." He had threatened to make us write a poem anyhow. Nothing like Claire's inscrutable, allusive verse. Mine was simple, maybe simple-minded, about Pittsburgh's famous crazy house,

Mayview—which I had never glimpsed and didn't even know its location, though it came up regularly in conversation. I never entered Rivera's classroom again. I never found out if Sean returned.

You talked about Mayview.
You predicted:
"You're going to drive me to Mayview."
Then you were driven there.
Someone drove you to Mayview.
You could also drive other people there.
You had to have a car.
You had to know how to drive.
You had to know how to be driven.
Once you arrived,
you swore that someone
had driven you there.
Sometimes you were ready
to be driven to Mayview.

The day of my month anniversary at Acme, Cover, Keith, and I lounged during lunch on the edge of an open bay, eating Munch's deviled crab, smoking cigarettes, when Danny appeared, very friendly, big smile, crummy teeth. He waved to us. His long flowing brown hair waved too in the late summer breeze—his enormous beard, his chain, jungle-bird shirt. Mellow as a guru. He asked Cover to pop up to his office.

Keith again trotted out his lavish strategy for winning back Bonnie. It now seemed like something that was happening to me and I really wanted it over with. I had grown up with Bonnie. We'd all been kids together, same school, same grade, same church: I and Claire, Keith and Bonnie. Then all the complications—new brains, new bodies, notions—when you stagger into one another's lives years later. I had been there at that hidden, little clinic when Bonnie had the abortion.

So, I said: "You know, Keith, I need to talk to you about getting back together with Bonnie." Open-ended enough, but my look and tone, unintentional, were enough, and it was immediately obvious how mystified and sad I'd made him, how I'd humiliated him. I realized then that he knew, better than anybody, what a dead-end, dumbass ploy he'd cooked up to win back Bonnie. But he needed me, above all people, regardless of the absurdity of his plan, to back him on this, to tell him *Full steam ahead, Brother.* Even though we both knew it was bullshit. He just looked at me, through me, really, like there was something behind me beckoning him, something he'd seen all along. That madhouse head of hair of his: if you fell into it, you'd be lost; you'd bleed to death.

"Keith," I said.

But then Cover was back and proclaimed, through a big smile, "Let's head for Sam and Ann's, boys, my treat."

"Aces, *compaesanos*," said Keith, on his feet, headed for the Mustang, sporting a bad wiry-headed maniac grin. "To the fucking bar."

Cover melodramatically floored it and executed six perfect doughnuts in the parking lot—a few other guys, dangling at lunch off the bays, wondering what the hell was up with him. A cloud of quartzite, gravel, and grit hovered them. Then he lit a doob, whipped the Mustang down Blue Run and, even though I felt hexed, the proposed trip to Sam and Ann's had considerably brightened the day. It did not occur to me that we would never see that warehouse again.

We walked into Sam and Ann's and ordered a pitcher of beer from ZZ-Top, who winked and palmed Cover a lid of weed for the Lionel train set Cover had fronted him. Cover backed us all up with two shots of Cuervo, and one for the barkeep—like launching a very serious session.

The three of us walked out on the dock, through the beat-up, rusty, busted-screen porch. About 12:30, the sun was on top of us, and I thought of Meursault. How he was seduced by the sun, the glare. The very light undid him. The blinding scrutiny. His sweating eyes.

You know: The *Can't fucking take it another instant* zenith. The loaded pistol. The Arab—with no name.

"To Acme," toasted Cover and lifted a shot.

We clinked glasses and threw back the Cuervo, chasing it with yellow beer in plastic cups, the light on the water bewitching.

"So what was up with that jagoff, Danny?" Keith asked.

"That jagoff, Danny, fired me."

Keith and I both said *What?* at the same time.

"Yeah," said Cover.

One night, for whatever reason, Danny had returned to the warehouse and swung in just as Cover was clambering out of the dumpster with contraband—in this case, microscopes. Danny hadn't stopped, just prowled off in the Pantera, very cool, no acknowledgment.

"This was two weeks ago," said Cover. "This is the kind of prick Danny is. Two weeks ago and, today, two weeks later, he calls me in to lower the boom; and, if he can, he'll withhold my last two weeks' pay, even though he didn't fire me two weeks ago. He said he can do it legally. Acme has lawyers. When I challenged him, he screamed at me to shut the fuck up. Stood up like he was going to pop me, foaming like a madman, and told me I better get down on my knees and kiss his fucking cowboy boots and thank God he was such a charitable fellow. If I said another word, he'd send my sorry ass to jail. He could do it and there was nobody in the world that would give enough of a shit to rescue a scumbag like me. I begged him not to turn me in to the law. I've had my share of go-rounds with the man over the years. Since I can remember, I've always been, like, this close"—Cover held his thumb and index finger an inch apart—"to catching time. I'm royally fucked, boys."

Keith and I gaped at him, this brand-new Cover, so suddenly metamorphosed, pondering what we could possibly say, then realizing with considerable panic, though it had been plain all along—like every other goddamn thing Keith and I had been trained to ignore—that we were Cover's accomplices, and were in trouble too. I wondered if I'd end up in jail—like Meursault, vermin scurrying over me as I slept, wondered if I should confess to Danny's fancy boots and beg forgiveness.

My mother would scream—*You ruined my life, same as getting knocked up*—if I caught a jolt, and cry and break things and the house would be a torture chamber for weeks. My dad would remain kind, respectful, would say what was on his mind. Words that would destroy us both because I'd left him no room but to say them—like knifing someone, like being knifed. Travis and Rita's hearts would explode; they would grieve like something out of Boccaccio.

Cover smiled the smile of the seasoned, embittered loser—the smile I envisioned cracking across Sisyphus's face every time he rammed his shoulder against his rock and began inching it back up the hill, that classic *fuck you* East Liberty smirk my mother affected when she was suffering more than anyone could possibly imagine, yet still going about her business.

"Don't worry, boys," he said. "I'm a scumbag, not a rat. I have my dignity. I won't tattle. And always remember: Danny caught me with microscopes. At least, I was fired for stealing educational toys."

He lifted his second Cuervo and said, "To Danny. I'll see about his fucking ass. I'll see about his fucking car too."

Keith and I knocked back the second shots to keep Cover company, and sipped beer. I was beyond relieved that he said he wouldn't rat, but I didn't feel out of the woods yet. I wanted to lam—from absolutely everything.

"Fuck Danny," Keith said. "Fuck everything."

The river gulped against the dock in green spangles. The sun was where it always perched, omniscient, judgmental, above our heads, in the high white sky. I shielded my eyes. The Cuervo and beer had leeched every bone from my body. Cover rolled two more numbers and dropped another bomb. This scrape with Danny—fired, docked two week's pay, the specter of the law—would prove the last straw with Hally. She had pledged to leave him just the night before. Take the kids. The marriage, fixing up that ramshackle relic of a house, a family, the garden: every bit of it was bullshit, a travesty—Hally's dream. She had a missionary complex, thought she could save him. Her parents, who had always hated Cover, had grubstaked them when they couldn't convince Hally to move back home with them, after he'd knocked her up with Star.

"What are you talking about?" Keith asked. *Paradise* had just detonated. Poor Keith sat in its shambles, sucked his cigarette through clenched teeth like biting on a stick, smoke and sunlight swirling about him, his eyes lasering into Cover.

"Fuck you," Cover said.

"No. What the fuck, Cover? Why'd you take us to your house then?"

"Because I wanted you to see it while it was still there. So fuck you. What about you? You better than me?" He lit both joints, handed one to Keith, and poured more beer in our cups. "Hally's a saint. Period. The kids are angels. She was always too good for me. I'm a fucking loser—my asshole job at the warehouse, embezzling toys, getting caught. I'm a fucking infant and a strung-out one."

Keith bored deeply into Cover, as if trying to interpret something—as if the words Cover had spoken were not as literal as the wrath of God. For a second, I thought he might jump Cover. I was overcome: *Paradise* had been an illusion. But isn't it always? Rivera had told us that Ernest Hemingway had claimed that stories are like icebergs, one-eighth visible, the rest submerged. I was attempting to think in this vein, to accord people their secret, underwater lives—maybe I had all along—but there was little comfort in acknowledging that all we can truly know of someone, even those we love and with whom we're most intimate, is a mere fraction.

As much as anything, I felt a fool at having been taken in—at how, only then, at Cover's awful revelation, I realized how desperately I had needed Cover and Hally's unlikely bargain to be real. To be love. I'd been snared in the same fantasy as Keith—that, maybe, everything I knew to be true, about myself, and Claire, and my parents, and Keith and Bonnie—that maybe there was some chance that things would turn out okay, that there was some chance, period.

What a chump dream fabricated by a chump East Liberty kid. There suddenly seemed no stab at a future, not a dead man's chance, no way of refashioning the world into a better place. My mother's *The Cruel World* had struck again. Yet I felt no resignation, no surrender, not even bitterness. I just felt sorry for myself. Where was my Sisyphean-Rita Schiaretta Sweeney scorn when I needed it? In our discussion about *The Stranger*, Rivera often brought up Camus's seeming ambivalence about life: *Is it or is it not worth living?* Which begged the question of suicide, what Camus had targeted as the sole "truly serious philosophical problem."

Keith flicked his cigarette into the river and dragged deeply on the weed. "Okay," he said, as he exhaled, then peeled off his T-shirt, kicked off his shoes and socks, and skinned out of his briefs and jeans.

I had been holding my breath and only then did I exhale as well. "What are you doing, Keith?" I asked.

"A little swim, Fritzy—to the other side."

"You're nuts, man. It's too far."

He ignored me, and turned to Cover. "Not nuts like this motherfucker. You coming, Cover?"

"Yeah," said Cover, peeling out of his clothes. "A little swim might be just the ticket."

Occasional boats clipped the sullen greenish-brown surface of the river, some towing water skiers, wakes V-ing out behind them, making their interminable way toward shore. But otherwise the water was flat, impenetrable as a mirror. The still, blinding sun bulged. I peered at the far shore, the other side. It swayed, mirage-like, in the rays' refraction off the water, and I had to look away, disoriented by sunspots, the booze, and reefer. What could possibly be over there? It had to be better than this falling-apart charade. But I had no idea how to get there, and I had never learned to swim.

Keith and Cover walked naked into the water until it reached their waists, and then they struck out, side by side, like Johnny Weissmuller, in *Tarzan*, like they had motors attached, arm over arm, silver water spraying magically about them. Too beautiful. Soon all I saw, through that searing light, were spouts of water nimbusing them as they swam far out into the Allegheny.

I baked, sipped beer, smoked a couple of cigarettes, and dozed off. When I opened my eyes, they were about halfway across, but still a long haul ahead. I don't know how long they'd been out there, but the sun, even hotter and brighter, hadn't moved, though it seemed much closer to earth. I took off my sweat-soaked shirt. It was pretty clear we'd be late as hell getting back to the warehouse, but I was so anesthetized and disoriented—*ennui*, right? —that I didn't give the slightest shit. Danny would raise hell, but I was going to get fired anyway. Today or in the coming days—it mattered little.

Keith and Cover, still side by side—they seemed to have slowed—suddenly stopped. Their heads bobbed on the water for moment. Maybe they exchanged words—I don't know—but Cover headed back toward Sam and Ann's. Keith remained stationary another second, then stroked again toward the other side, and I lost sight of him.

"Keith," I screamed, jumped up and stripped to my underwear and tennis shoes. "Keith," I screamed again. Thunder replied, rolling down the Allegheny, off the mighty Ohio, from the far west, yet that sun still torched the sky. I caught sight of Keith again, halos of spindrift where he cut the water, but he was too far away to determine if he had turned back or was still headed for the distant bank.

I waded into the tepid murk, step by step, until I hit the sludge. It oozed into my shoes, and grabbed my ankles. To my chest, I breaststroked as if swimming, propelling myself forward, as I trudged, unsuctioning each quick-sanded shoe until I simply stepped out of them. The water admitted me as if it had been waiting a long time, and I went under.

I opened my eyes. Maudlin carp, mutated to monsters by toxins, eyed me clairvoyantly. With me were Keith and Cover, Travis and Rita, Claire, even Camus and Rivera; and all those stiffs at the warehouse, their names stitched across the breast pockets of their Acme uniforms. I understood how easily one is absorbed, suffocated, by one's own yearning—how seductive, how tranquil, it can be—and suddenly all I craved was to succumb to that slumber, and ever so slowly I began to sink. The sun magnified itself across the ceiling of the river. Brooches of light fell across my face. I reached for them, and pulled them to me, one after the other, and finally gasped to the surface.

But the sun had vanished. In its place, darkness pressed the water—as if the day had passed since I'd gone under. Choking, barefoot, I thrashed the muck for shore, spitting poison water. When I was to my thighs, I turned again to the river. The glassy surface swayed, out of kilter, as if it might tip. Mist swept over it. Thunder sounded again. Cover was about fifty yards out, flailing, stopping every minute to catch his breath, tread water, go under, bob back up. I ventured a few more yards back into the river to coax Cover in, but the river had swollen. It pitched toward me in waves, clouds like blast furnaces churning low, shape-shifting on the whistling wind. Another step and I'd be over my head again, and there would be no more *Again*. No more *Before*. Only everlasting *After*.

Cover, mere meters from me, stopped swimming, caught my eye for one rueful instant, then disappeared. I lurched a foot, then another, another, inching into *After*, groping for him beneath the roiling river. It was in my mouth, over my nose, at my eyes—when Cover stood, simply stood, heaving, weeping, his long hair aged, gaunt, eyes white, skeletal. I muscled him toward the dock. The river shoved us—dragged down by the bog that clamped our feet—back out, back in, until we made the ladder, and I held him there a moment, and finally dragged him three rungs to the deck where he collapsed. Sam and Ann's was abandoned, no lights, no ZZ Top, the door into the bar, in the gale, banging back and forth in its jamb.

I scanned the river for Keith. The sky was black. The river was black. It had begun to rain, steady, silvery. What would I tell them—Mike and Theresa Gentile, Travis and Rita, Claire, even Isabella? The first blast of lightning spidered the firmament and detonated. The dock quaked. Then another massive crackling blast illuminated the river for miles in frayed lacy cables and lit up the distant bank. There stood Keith, on the other side, naked, arms lifted—in triumph, praise. Surrender. As if the lightning ascending from his electrocuted hair into the heavens—as if the very light—issued from him.

ACKNOWLEDGMENTS

First and foremost, Joan Carey Bathanti and Jacob and Beckett Bathanti for the love and care that has fueled me these many years and in the writing of this book. Great thanks to Marie, my one and only sister in all senses of the word. To Anthony Mannella, who inspired much of this book. To the following little muses who bring me such joy: Leo and Sam Burgess; Rodman, Davy and Sterling Frazier; Joshua Reese; Maxwell and Emerson Liberty; and Gavin Phillips. To Appalachian State University and especially the Department of Interdisciplinary Studies. To Agnes Gambill for her invaluable help and advice in navigating permissions. And lasting and profound gratitude to Regal House Publishing for bringing out this book: wonderful Pam Van Dyk and especially Jaynie Royal for seeing it to the finishing line with such grace and elegance.